Blazing Sands

Book 7 – The San Capistrano Series

by

Angelique Jurd

COPYRIGHT

DEDICATION PAGE

For May, Penny, Tom, and Lauren

For getting this over the finish line.

1

If Alex doesn't move, perhaps the person jabbing the small, pointy finger into his bicep will go away. Unlikely, but he can hope. Maybe if he just plays possum...

The corner of the book covering his face is lifted. "Daddy, you awake?"

"Nope."

"How come you're talking if you're not awake?"

"Magic."

"Nu-uh."

He opens one eye to peer at his daughter. "Smarty paws."

Lucy giggles.

"See? Told you. You are too awake." She scrambles up beside him and stretches out, so they're eye to eye. "At Henry's house we saw a movie about dinosaurs."

"Yeah? Did you like it?" Alex tries to think what dinosaur movies would be appropriate for a five-year-old.

"Yeah, there was this dinosaur called Little Foot and his mommy died."

He breathes a sigh of relief; he knows that one. It's animated. As Lucy continues to chatter about her afternoon at Henry's, he drifts off again, lulled by the sound of her voice.

"Daddy?"

"Hmmmm?"

"What dinosaurs were around when you were a little boy?"

With that, he's wide awake. What dinosaurs indeed!

He marks his place in the book and swings his legs around, lifting Lucy up with him as he stands. She's really too tall to be carried now, but he enjoys it anyway.

"There were no dinosaurs when I was a little boy, Lulubug." Not unless you count my mother, he thinks.

"Not even trynasaws?"

"Tyrannosaurs? No, not even tyrannosaurs." Kissing her cheek, he shoulders the door to the kitchen open. "But you should ask Papa. He's older than me and he might have seen some."

"Some what?"

Ben leans out from the pantry, points to a bag of groceries on the counter, and makes a grabby motion. Alex passes them to him.

"Dinosaurs. Lulubug wants to know how many you saw when you were a little boy."

Confusion clouds Ben's gaze.

"Come again? Dinosaurs?"

"Yeah." Lucy slithers down Alex's side and follows Ben into the pantry. "Daddy said there weren't any when he was a little boy. Not even trynasaws. But he said you might have seen some 'cause you're older than him."

"Oh, did he just?" Ben looks over the tops of the glasses he now wears most of the time, and Alex blows him a kiss. "I hate to disappoint you both, but there were absolutely no dinosaurs when I was a little boy."

"Awww, that's no fun." Lucy pouts. "Can I have a cookie?"

"Nope, but you can have a banana." Alex folds his arms and leans against the counter. "Why don't you go find your sister and Bart and we can go for a walk."

Protesting that bananas are dumb, Lucy does as she's bid. Alex chews his lip and fights a grin when Ben comes out of the pantry and places his hands on the counter, either side of Alex's hips.

"Dinosaurs, huh?"

"Hey, not my fault you're older than me." He dips his head and brushes a quick kiss over Ben's mouth. "They watched a dinosaur movie at Henry's. For an awful minute, I thought she meant one of the Jurassic ones."

Ben snorts. "You don't have to worry about that one, she'd be fine. Ally might be a little scared, but not Lulu." He puts the milk away. "Besides, Jurassic Park is a classic now. Hardly scary at all."

Alex rolls his eyes. Reaches for the bag of fruit and pulls out a bunch of bananas.

"Well, how about we wait a little before we introduce these particular classics, okay?" He puts four bananas on the counter and gets Bart's leash from the hook. "Next you'll be wanting to show her *Jaws*. Or *Halloween*"

"Nah, she needs to be at least ten before she watches *Halloween*." Ben grins and hums the theme from *Jaws*. He picks up a banana and waggles it in Alex's direction. "You know, these are giving me an idea for later."

"Everything gives you an idea for later."

"It's why you love me."

"Keep telling yourself that."

Ben pulls him closer and nuzzles at the spot under his ear. Alex flinches at the tickle and laughs.

This is how weekends are supposed to be, he thinks. Quiet and happy.

The door from the living room crashes open; Bart bounds in, followed by the girls.

"*Ew, Dads!* Enough with the smushy stuff." Ally wrinkles her nose and flips her blond hair over her shoulder. "I thought we were going for a walk. Can I have a cookie?"

"Banana." Alex points to the fruit and clips the leash on Bart's collar.

"See? Told you he said no." Lucy grabs her own piece of fruit and darts outside, followed by Ally.

Alex opens his mouth to tell them to get their jackets, that it's a little cool, but they're already gone. Sighing, he pulls his own jacket on, then grabs both garments from their hooks, and waits for Ben.

"When," Ben tugs the zipper up, "did we stop being Papa and Daddy and become Dads?"

"About the same time that she decided she didn't want to take Mister Snuffles to bed with her anymore." He waits with Bart while Ben steps into the courtyard. Checks he has his key, then pulls the kitchen door shut and locks it.

"Wait. What? When did she give up Mister Snuffles? Where was I?"

The girls are waiting near the water, bent over hunting for shells.

Alex kisses his cheek. "You've been busy." They walk down to the water's edge and he hands the girls their jackets.

"Left or right, troops?"

2

Stretched out on the sofa, only half watching the movie they've chosen, Ben rubs his hand over Alex's hip. Loves the feel of Alex's body against his like this. He picks up his glass of wine and takes a sip, then offers it to Alex, who shakes his head and shifts a little. The movement sends a pleasant shiver through him.

"Lulu's getting so tall."

Alex nods. Smothers a yawn against Ben's chest. "Yeah, she's nearly out of her new jeans already."

"Henry's mom is expecting again."

"Really? Didn't they just have a baby?"

Ben shrugs. "Not really, she's nearly two. Remember when the girls were babies?" He picks up the remote and thumbs the volume down. "I kind of miss that, don't you?"

"Which part? The diapers? Or the sleepless nights?"

"It wasn't that bad."

Alex tips his head back and gives him an upside-down smirk. "What about the lack of sex?"

Okay, yes that might be a valid point, but... it's not like they're doing much in that department at the moment with his workload anyway.

Headlights sweep across the room, followed a few seconds later by car doors shutting.

"They're early." Alex picks up the glass this time and sips; Ben takes it from him and has another mouthful. When the door opens, Bart sits up in his basket, tail thumping.

"Kristen Stewart is a badass," Jamie announces as he drops into the corner armchair and pulls Leo onto his lap. "She took this dude out – like just wiped him off his feet – using a motorbike. It was so awesome. I am so going to be Kristen Stewart when I grow up."

"You can't be Stewart, you dork." Leo grins and pulls a strand of Jamie's hair. He stretches one leg out and knocks a framed photograph off the coffee table with his foot. "Ooops."

"Why? Because she's a chick?"

"No, because she likes chicks and you don't."

"I do like chicks," Jamie protests. "I just don't want to f-"

"Okay, we get the picture." Alex stands and gathers up the empty popcorn bowl and wine glasses. "Kristen Stewart is badass. I take it you enjoyed the movie."

"Yup. It was freakin' awesome."

"Staying the night, Leo?" Ben stretches. Rubs at the twinge in his back.

"Yeah, if that's okay. My sisters are having a sleepover so there isn't going to be any sleep in my house tonight."

"Not likely to be any here either, if the past is anything to go by," Ben mutters as Alex moves toward the kitchen. Nobody seems to have heard the comment. Or they're ignoring him; he's not sure which.

"Volvo's making that clunky noise again."

The old Volvo they'd passed on to Jamie has been making intermittent knocking sounds lately and Ben is starting to wonder if the time has come to retire it. He makes a mental note to call their garage on Monday and book it in.

"Okay, we'll see if Roger can take it during the week."

From the kitchen he hears the sound of the door to the courtyard opening; Alex letting Bart out. They won't be long since the Labrador seems to have reached the stage of canine middle age, where he's happy to venture no further than the edge of the sand at this time of night.

"How's college, Leo? Home for long?"

"Just the weekend. It's okay. I like my sociology course, that's pretty cool."

"Miss home?" Ben turns off the television, knowing the boys won't be staying out here once he and Alex head upstairs.

"Miss Mom's cooking; cafeteria food is pretty crap." He kisses Jamie's cheek. "Miss this dork."

Bart pads back in. Goes straight to the stairwell and waits, front paws on the bottom step. Seconds later, Alex joins them. "There's some left-over pie in the fridge if you guys want it. Just make sure you put your dishes in the dishwasher. Sleep well."

"Sleep." Ben chuckles. "Yeah, whatever."

"Dad!" Jamie glares at Ben, then turns to Alex. "Could you control your husband?"

"If I knew how to do that, kid, don't you think I would have done it by now?" Alex gives him a gentle shove toward the stairs. "Come on you, bed."

***

"I was thinking we could let them use the apartment next year." Ben leans against the bathroom door, holding his toothbrush up to his mouth.

Alex glances up from his book. "Huh?"

"I figure the chances of him choosing UCLA are pretty high given that Leo's already there. We could let them use the apartment rather than rent some student dive. I mean it's sort of why we bought it, isn't it? What do you think?"

Alex places the book on his nightstand; rubs his eyes. "Well, I thought we bought it as an investment and to have somewhere to stay in the city. I also think you're getting ahead of yourself. He hasn't even decided what he wants to do yet, let alone where he wants to do it."

"Well, yeah, but he's already doing Leo, and I think it's a safe bet that he wants to *continue* doing Leo, so you know..."

Alex squints and points his finger at Ben. "Knock it off, or I can promise you you'll be swapping places with Bart for the night. Do you really have to tease him *every* time Leo stays over?"

Ben grins. "Ah come on, the whole point of having a teenager is to embarrass them, right?"

"I'll take your word for it."

Alex's tone is light enough, but Ben knows what's going through his mind. He winks. "You do that, baby."

He turns back to the bathroom counter and finishes brushing his teeth. Rinses. Smooths moisturizer over his face, careful not to look at the scar on his chest.

"I'd like to see you try that on Lulu in a few years." Alex sidles in beside him and reaches for his toothbrush. Ben kisses his cheek and leaves him to his routine. He suspects that when they're seventy, Alex will still have privacy issues. Not that he can blame him, he supposes.

"Has he said anything to you about what he might be interested in?" he asks as he pulls the curtains.

Jamie's grades are good and he's even holding his own in the subjects he hates-algebra, history, and Spanish. They've asked him once or twice if he has any ideas for college, but each time he's dodged the question.

"I wouldn't be surprised if he opts for something artistic."

Ben nods to himself. "Yeah, I think that's on the cards."

In the corner of the room is the old armchair they used to sit in when the girls were babies and wouldn't settle at night. It was the chair his mother had used when he was a baby. Ben drops into it now with a sigh. Picks at a piece of the stuffing escaping through a worn seam and grins to himself as he runs his fingers absently over the surgery scar hidden beneath his shirt. Some nights he feels like he's old enough for *his* stuffing to escape his seams.

Not tonight though.

Tonight, he just feels happy and secure in the routine of his life. His family. Knowing the kids are happy and safe, asleep - or not, he thinks with a wry grin - in the house he grew up in. That he and Alex are as good together as they've ever been. Bart turns a circle in his basket before flopping down with a soft woof. Even Dork Dog seems content with life.

He's lost in his musings when the bathroom door opens and Alex comes out, blue pajama pants low on his hips. Forty in a few months, he's still lean, belly muscles taut beneath the light trail of hair. Ben lets his gaze wander up Alex's body. Smiles at the eternity symbol tattooed just above his heart with his, Ben's, name linking the ends. Broad shoulders on which rests the familiar shaggy tumble of chestnut curls, still not showing any gray. Strong, muscular neck. When he reaches Alex's face, he's met with a smile.

"Enjoying yourself?"

"Very much."

"Idiot."

The word is softened with love and Ben grins, tongue caught between his teeth. "Idiot who loves you."

Shaking his head, Alex approaches and straddles him. A knee either side of Ben's thighs. Heat shivers through him.

"Yeah?"

"Yeah."

"Good thing I love you back then, isn't it?"

Ben pulls Alex toward him. Presses a kiss to his mouth and thrills a little at the soft warmth of his lips.

"Where do we stand on the whole removal of pajama pants question?" he asks.

"I think we can work something out." Alex kisses him again; firmer this time. "Assuming you can stay awake."

As it happens, he can.

3

Ben taps the clicker and waits for the garage door to descend. He's not sure why they waited so long to install automatic doors. Nostalgia? Misplaced loyalty to his mother's original design? Who knows? What he does know is that on days like today - days when he's been in court for eleven hours for the third day straight - he feels every minute of his forty-three years. He rubs his hand over this chest, over the scar, pockets the clicker, and makes his way along the side of the house.

As he turns the corner, he's met by Bart, chasing some smell along the trail from the beach. His tail bounces back and forth as if it's on a spring. Seemingly intent on whatever he's sniffing, he walks into Ben's legs.

"Need to borrow my glasses, Dork Dog?" Smiling, he scratches the Labrador's ears.

Alex comes through the gate from the beach and dips his head to accept a kiss.

"Good walk?" Ben winds his arm around his waist. Stifles a yawn.

"He got spooked by a lump of driftwood, so we didn't get far. He's not doing so good at night these days."

"Kids asleep?"

"Yeah, but I have instructions to cover you in hugs and kisses."

Ben holds the door open. "Oh, now that's something I can get behind." He waggles his eyebrows as Alex passes him. Laughs at the eye-roll it earns him.

He drops his briefcase on the floor and goes to the fridge for a bottle of beer, twists the cap off and drinks half of the bottle in a single mouthful. Smothers a belch behind his hand.

Alex raises an eyebrow as he opens the oven door. The rich, heady aroma of roasting beef fills the kitchen. "That bad?"

Ben rubs his temple, eyes shut. "You have no idea. Bill Langley called and asked if I would go up and meet with him and Aaron Crawford. They have something they want to discuss."

"What?"

Ben spreads his hands in a 'search me' gesture. "No idea."

"He didn't give you any clue?"

"Nope."

"Any guesses?"

"None at all."

"Business or personal?"

Putting his beer on the counter, Ben washes his hands. "What part of 'I have no idea' was I not being clear about babe?"

Alex scowls. "Didn't you ask?"

Ben kisses him and takes his beer back to the table. "Of course I asked. They said they want to discuss whatever it is in person. You know as much as I do. God, that smells good. Court salads suck. And not in the good way.".

Alex chuckles. "I'm not sure if I should be proud of you for choosing a salad or concerned about what you want to do with it."

Ben shrugs off his coat. Hangs it up, retrieves his briefcase, and sits down with a sigh. "Trust me, you have no reason to be jealous of a salad."

"Why would Dad be jealous of a salad?" Jamie lets the living room door swing shut behind him.

Ben takes in the black boots, black leather kilt, and bright yellow t-shirt, the carefully made-up eyes, and grins. Jamie follows his gaze with his own.

"What?" He kisses Ben's cheek and drops onto the chair next to him. Ben opens his mouth to answer, but Alex's voice cuts him off.

"Whatever you're about to say, don't."

"Can I have one of those?" Jamie nods at the bottle next to Ben's plate.

"Sure."

"School night." Alex puts a plate in front of each of them and returns to the stove for his own.

Ben offers Jamie an apologetic smile, but it seems neither of them has the energy to argue. He turns his attention to more important topics.

"Homework done?"

"Yep. And I've put the trash out. And yes, you can see the floor in my room."

Ben looks at Alex. "Who is this and what have they done with Jamie?"

"Wants to go to a concert with Leo on Saturday." Alex takes his place at the table and reaches for the jug of water.

"And?" A date rarely merits a pre-emptive strike of chores and room tidying. Unless...

"Up in L.A.," Alex adds.

There it is.

Ben sips his beer and studies Jamie for a moment. In the big scheme of things, the request isn't that unusual. After all, the kid is nearly nineteen, will graduate in a few months, and come the end of next summer will be starting college himself. Asking their permission to go to a concert will be a thing of the past. Ben pushes the thought away.

"Alcohol?" he asks.

"Not even beer." Jamie's cheeks flame scarlet, but he doesn't drop his gaze.

Ben considers teasing him a little over the incident last summer, but a head shake from Alex changes his mind.

"Transport?"

Jamie has his full permit - has had it for a month - and loves to drive but Ben isn't sure about driving all the way up to Los Angeles.

"I could take the bus, I don't mind."

At the other end of the table, Alex smiles and busies himself with his plate.

"Who are you seeing?"

"Billie Eilish."

"I… have no clue who that is, but I'm guessing they're cool." Ben chews a chunk of the roast beef. It's as good as it smells. Swallows. "Staying?"

"At the dorm, I guess."

Ben thinks this over for a moment, then puts his fork down.

"How about this? I have to go up to L.A. on Friday anyway, we could all go up and stay at the apartment. See Uncle Matt and Aunt Claire. That way you guys can stay there."

Jamie's face lights up. "Really? We could do that?"

Ben looks at Alex, who nods. "Why not? We could all use a weekend off."

A weekend away will do them all good, and a change of scenery could be just what he needs in order to unravel the final stages of this damned case. If he can get a continuation until Monday, he might even have it finished by Friday and have the weekend off.

"Are you sure you're going to be able to get away?" Alex asks. "You've been late every ni-"

Jamie's phone chirps. Despite Alex's protest, he pulls the device from his pocket and looks at the screen.

"Fuck!"

"Hey!"

Ben peers over the top of his glasses, first at the protesting Alex, and then at Jamie. "What's wrong?"

"There's another fucking fire!"

Alex's fork clatters against his plate. "Oh God. Where?" He reaches for his own phone, checking, Ben knows, to see if he's been called in by either one of the clinics he works with or if the emergency room, short-staffed at the best of times, needs him to help.

Judging by his lack of reaction, Ben guesses not.

"Applesby Avenue. The Masters' house. I have algebra with Maree. *Fuck!* This is the third fucking one! I hope they're okay."

"Can we dial back the f-bombs?" Alex asks without looking up from his phone. There's no heat in his words, and Ben can tell it's habit rather than a true reprimand.

Jamie looks from one to the other; distress clouds his blue eyes. "Dad, is there anything we can do to help? Can we go and see if they're okay? They could stay here, couldn't they?"

The question is directed at Alex, who rests his elbow on the table. His voice is gentle but firm when he answers.

"The last thing the fire department needs right now is us getting in the way, but we'll make some calls and anything we can do, we will do. I haven't been called in to Emergency or the clinics, so that's a good sign."

Ben rubs Jamie's arm. "Dad's right. We need to let the emergency services do their jobs and then we can see how we can help, okay?"

"What happens if they can't save the house? All the others burned down."

That question, Ben knows, is for him. "Hopefully they've got good insurance and it won't take long to get them sorted." He glances at Alex. "Finish up your dinner then we'll make some calls."

"But..."

"Jamie, I know you're worried, but the last thing the people dealing with this need right now is us bothering them, okay? Don't worry, we'll call."

***

"Thanks, Frank. Would you mind letting them know that if there's anything we can do to help, not to hesitate? Great." Ben hangs up and turns to Alex. "They were out to dinner, so the place was empty, thank God."

"House?"

Ben shakes his head. "Couldn't save it. Frank says it's the same set up as the others and that they're definitely looking at a serial arsonist."

"Someone's deliberately burning houses down?" Tucked into the beanbag, hugging his knees, Jamie glances from Ben to Alex and back again. "What will happen to them? Maree's family, I mean."

Ben sits down next to Alex. "It will take them a while to get things sorted out, but San Cap's a small community and it takes care of people. They're with family for now though, which is the best possible place for them."

Alex sips his tea, seemingly lost in thought. Ben rubs his arm.

"You okay, baby?" he asks, saddened when Jamie doesn't tease him for the endearment.

"Yeah, I'm fine." He frowns over his coffee cup. "Do you think we should get *our* alarms and things checked?"

"What?" Jamie looks up at them, eyes wide with concern. "Us? Why would someone burn down our house?"

Alex stretches his leg out and rubs his foot against Jamie's calf. "Shhh. You'll wake the girls. I'm sure we're fine. I'm just saying that it might be a good time to update our own security."

"But-"

Ben takes his glasses off and rubs his eyes. It's not a terrible idea and if they're going to go up to the city to the apartment, he may as well arrange for that to be checked as well. He pulls his phone from his pocket and adds CALL MAXINE to his list for the next day.

God, he's getting as bad as Alex with his lists but if he doesn't write it down, he'll forget. In the back of his mind he can hear Polly laughing and telling him that getting old ain't for sissies. An elbow in his ribs gets his attention.

"Did you hear what I just said?"

"Um... depends."

A smile flits across Alex's face. "On?"

"How much trouble I'll be in if I say no."

Alex rolls his eyes. "I said Ally's teacher called to say she's having trouble seeing the board."

"Who is? Miss Lassiter?"

Jamie sniggers, but Alex looks less amused.

"No, you idiot. Ally. I made sure I was paying attention this afternoon, and she gets quite close to the television and the computer screen and says they're fuzzy if she doesn't. I also got her to read to me and she had to hold the book about here." He holds his hand an inch from the tip of his nose. "Have you noticed anything?"

Ben shakes his head. Frowns. "No. Do you think she needs glasses?"

"Maybe. Or it could be a habit, but I think we need to check it anyway."

"When's the appointment?" It's a not question of *has* Alex made one but of *when* he's made it for.

"Tomorrow afternoon. Four-thirty."

"Okay, I should be done for the day. Want me to take her or pick up Lucy?"

For the next fifteen minutes they iron out the details of the coming week. Finally, Alex calls Bart and takes the empty mugs to the kitchen. Ben puts a hand out to help Jamie to his feet.

"Go ahead and grab the tickets for your show; we can swing past the dorm and pick Leo up when we get there. Might even go check out Mickey and friends on Sunday and yes, he can come too if he wants." He winks. "Or you can hang out at the apartment for the day."

Jamie groans and shakes his head. "You are such a freak."

"Why do you think Dad loves me?" He gives the teenager a gentle shove. "Go to bed."

4

"Daddy?" Ally presses against his leg, the way she used to when she was little. When something unnerved her.

"Yeah, monster?"

"Do I have to wear the glasses?"

Alex's heart sinks. He and Ben had explained to her this morning that glasses would stop things being fuzzy and help her see things better. That reading would be fun again, and she wouldn't have to sit so close to things to see them. When he'd picked her up from school, they'd talked in the car about what would happen at the appointment and she had seemed okay.

At least he'd thought she had.

Ever since his mother snatched the girls and abandoned Ally, beaten and drugged in a motel room, there's been a cautiousness to her that tugs at his heart. It had worsened after Ben's heart attack, but Alex had thought it was improving. The way she's pressing her forehead against his thigh and refusing to look up at him tells him he was wrong.

He crouches, and with the tip of his finger, tilts her chin up.

"Baby girl, what's wrong?"

Tears fill her eyes. "What if the kids at school laugh at me or call me names?"

He wraps his arms around her and lifts her up. Tries to remember the last time he picked her up and carried her anywhere while she was awake. She's nearly nine now, with babyhood well behind her. Wisps of blond hair frame her face; he can see echoes of Ben in her green eyes and the set of her jaw. Of her great grandmother, Polly, too. More and more often though he sees her namesake and grandmother, Allie, in the tilt of her head and the shape of her face.

Lately she's been protesting anything that strikes her as a nod to being a 'baby' and Alex half expects her to squirm out of his arms, but she buries her face in the dip of his shoulder. He sits in a nearby chair and rocks her for a moment, the way he used to after a nightmare.

After his mother.

"Ally, look at me." She shakes her head and huddles closer. He rests his cheek against her head and lowers his voice. "Nobody is going to make fun of you. Lara and Jack in your class both wear glasses. Papa wears glasses. Aunt Claire wears glasses for reading. And you know what?"

Ally says nothing, but he can tell by the way she holds herself that she's listening.

"Your Grandma Allie wore glasses too."

She leans back to squint at him.

"Papa's mommy?"

"Yeah. She had pink glasses. You look just like her, you know, so we could see if they have some pink ones that you like." He smiles, hoping to reassure her. "You'll be able to show Aunt Claire and Uncle Matt on Saturday."

Something in his words seems to hit a note with her and her face lights up.

"Maybe I could just wear them when I read things. And the rest of the time I can take them off. Like Aunt Claire does."

She looks so hopeful that Alex hates what he has to say next.

"I'm sorry honey, Doctor Harris says you have to wear them all the time."

"But Daddy, why?" Her lower lip trembles.

"Because the thing that needs help in your eyes is different to the thing in Aunt Claire's. Papa wears his all the time now too."

"Will Lulu have to get glasses?"

Alex sighs. "I don't know." Then because he can't stand the sadness in her face, he adds. "Maybe. Sweetheart, it's going to be fine. We're going to choose some really pretty ones with Doctor Harris and then we'll go home, and you can tell Papa all about them."

"Okay." To his surprise, she makes no attempt to move but remains in his lap. "Daddy?"

"Mmmmm?"

"Can we get some ice cream to take home?"

Alex chuckles and kisses the tip of her nose. "You are your Papa's daughter. I guess we can, but you have to make sure Papa doesn't eat too much."

"Okay. Do you think they have purple ones? Purple glasses might be okay, I guess."

He sets her on the ground and stands. "Let's go find out."

***

"Do you think we need to worry about the munchkin?"

Alex thinks for a moment. "No. I don't think there'll be any problems with the other kids, and I'll talk to Miss Lassiter in the morning. She'll be fine once she's used to them." He plugs his phone into the charger on the nightstand. Gets into bed and shimmies over to rest his head on Ben's chest. "I spoke to Claire today, and it's all good for the weekend. She said the girls could stay with them Saturday night if they want."

"We're going to need two cars to bring back all the toys and clothes, aren't we?"

"Probably." Alex closes his eyes; lets Ben's words wash over him in the dark as he drifts toward sleep.

"Jasper's mom was there when I picked up Lulu. She's had the twins. Little boys. Cute little things." He rubs Alex's forearm. "You ever think about having another one?"

Alex's eyes snap open, sleep forgotten. When Ben had mentioned another baby the other day, he'd brushed it off as a joke. Maybe he wasn't kidding around.

"Are you serious?"

Heavy silence fills the room, broken only by the sound of Bart shifting in his basket.

"I don't know. Maybe." Alex waits for him to continue. "I'm not saying right this minute-"

"Well, that's good."

"Bite me. I don't know. With Jamie probably heading off to college in the fall and Ally turning ten next year. Hell, she's already given up Mister Snuffles. It might be nice." He sighs. "Maybe I'm just having a midlife crisis."

Alex swallows a bubble of laughter and kisses his chest. "I guess it's better than suddenly discovering leather and wanting me to call you Daddy."

"You mean that's an option?"

"Idiot." Then to be sure Ben doesn't pursue the idea, adds "and no, it's not."

"Spoilsport."

"You have about three minutes before I fall asleep, sweetheart, so how about we get back to babies."

"I remember a time when the subject made you vomit."

"Two minutes. And counting."

"Look, I don't really know what I'm saying, except maybe it's something we could talk about?"

Alex shuffles up and kisses Ben's cheek. Closes his eyes again.

"Talking works."

5

Hands in his pockets, Ben looks out the window of Bill Langley's office at the street below. Alex and the kids are picking up Leo, and they'll all meet back at the apartment before heading over to the restaurant for dinner later. Matt has promised something delicious for dessert, which hopefully means chocolate cheesecake. And brownies to take home on Sunday after they've been to see Mickey.

The lighting in the office casts a part reflection on the window. He uses it to adjust his tie. The violet silk gives a subtle touch of color to the charcoal Armani suit and shirt he's chosen. Light glints off the gold frame of his glasses.

"Ben." Billy Langley's reflection appears next to his in the glass and Ben turns to greet him. "Sorry to keep you waiting."

Ben accepts his former boss's outstretched hand with a grin. "No problem. I haven't been here long. How are things?"

"Can't complain, can't complain at all. How are Alex and the family?"

"Alex is great. He's nearly completed his degree in counseling and has an offer already to set up in a practice in San Cap. Jamie's a senior, so we're starting to look at colleges for him and the girls are growing like weeds. Ally will be in double digits next year and already has eye rolling down to a fine art."

The old man grins. "Wait until she hits her teens."

"Yeah, I think I'm going to put in a request to defer that."

"You do that. I'll be waiting to hear how it went." Langley gestures to an armchair. "Take a seat, Aaron is on his way up. That man is never on time for anything. How Cheryl hasn't strangled him yet, I don't know. Can I get you something to drink? Coffee? Scotch?"

In his head, Ben hears Alex suggest water or tea. He loves the man, God knows, but that is not how you do business in this city.

"Whatever you're having is fine."

"Scotch it is."

By the time Langley has poured three glasses of Scotch, Aaron has arrived. Hands have been shaken, social niceties exchanged and they each take a seat. Langley is in his sixties now. Well liked, well respected, and wealthy, he's worked hard to get his firm where it is and Ben admires his dedication and determination. Aaron Crowley is a little younger–late fifties if Ben's memory serves him–and has long been the fashionable face of the firm. Quick witted, charming, and well connected, he's always been very public about preferring to work on the business than in it.

They make a formidable team.

"So, what can I do for you, gentlemen?" Ben asks. They've gone through all the expected social hoops; he sees no reason to beat around the proverbial bush. He has a family and hopefully a chocolate cheesecake waiting for him.

Crawford crosses his legs and clasps his hands. "Ben, we've been looking to expand the firm, and we'd like to make you a proposition."

"Oh."

"We'd like to buy your practice."

The Scotch catches in Ben's throat; he coughs to clear it. "Excuse me?"

"You were–are–an excellent lawyer. You were our youngest Junior Partner and you have done an extraordinary job building your own firm. We think together we could create something special."

Perplexed, Ben frowns. His practice is certainly successful, but it's not big. There's only him and Fiona and a couple of younger lawyers he calls on if needed.

"Yes, but you have built a solid reputation down in San Cap that has been noticed up here." Langley tents his fingers under his chin. "It's only going to be a matter of time before someone else tries to make a move on you. We have history; we wanted to be the first."

"I'm very flattered, but I d-"

Langley holds his hand up, halting the words. "Before you finish that statement, let us tell you our offer, then you can take it away. Talk to Alex about it. Think it over."

"Bill, I-"

"We'd like to offer you two hundred and fifty thousand dollars and a full partnership. Name over the door. *Crawford, Langley, and Larsen.* How does that sound?"

A quarter of a million dollars and a full partnership. That's a… lot. Of everything.

"You want me to move my practice back to the city?"

"We would look at opening an office in San Capistrano since that is where you're established, but obviously it would be ideal if you were available to the wider firm as well. You still have an apartment here I believe."

"Yeah. Yeah we do." Ben tries to gather his thoughts. "Look, I'm not sure what to say to be honest. It's an amazing offer but the kids are settled in school and we've been talking about maybe having another baby and–"

Amusement glitters in Crawford's eyes. "As Bill said, you can continue to be based in San Capistrano, but you do know there are schools here in L. A., right?"

Tempting though it is, Ben decides that flipping off a man who has just offered him two hundred and fifty thousand dollars is probably not a great idea.

Instead, he smiles.

"Of course I do, it's just I…" Unsure what to say, he lets the words trail off. "I don't know what to say."

"Look, all we're asking is that you hear the rest of our proposition and talk it over with Alex for a few days, then come back to us, maybe this time next week. We're open to a counteroffer." Crawford's tone is even. Gives nothing away.

"And," Bill Langley adds, "if you decide it isn't something you're interested in, we will respect that." He takes a deep breath. "But I very much hope that you *will* be interested, Ben. As I said, you're an excellent lawyer."

***

"*How much?*" Alex stops buttoning his shirt and stares at Ben.

"You heard. Quarter of a million and a full partnership."

Alex sinks onto the bed, disbelief draining his cheeks of color. Ben can relate to the feeling.

"That's a lot of fucking money, Ben."

"Yes. Yes, it is."

"Are you considering it?"

Ben crouches in front of Alex and takes his hand. "I've said I'll talk it over with you for the next few days and go back to them next Friday. It's not just up to me, baby."

Alex bites his lip.

"I appreciate that, but it's also your career. Is this something you've thought about? Something you want?"

"Alex, I don't know. I like our life. Our family. This would change things–and not all of it would be for the better. I'd be working long hours."

"You already work long hours." Alex looks down at his hands.

"Exactly. This wouldn't make that any better. But, on the other hand, we'd be financially secure for the rest of our lives and so would the kids. Not that we're in a bad position now but this would open up a whole lot of new possibilities. Things we could offer them."

"I thought you wanted to have another baby?"

"The two things aren't mutually exclusive."

"No, I know but you just said you'd be working more."

"Yeah and I also said that the decision isn't just mine. I told them we'd talk about it, so let's do that. Talk. Figure it out like we always do. Bill said they're open to a counteroffer, so maybe that's something we should think about."

"Counteroffer?"

Ben decides it's time to put the subject aside for the moment. "Baby, we don't need to make a decision right now, okay? Let's go have dinner. Matt said there's dessert."

6

"We helped Uncle Matt make a cake, and we watched *Lilo and Stitch*, and Aunt Claire said we can have waffles for breakfast."

Alex smiles at the iPad screen. Apparently, Lucy hadn't been able to wait for Claire to finish combing her damp hair to start FaceTime. His smile widens when Claire reminds her to stop squirming for the third time in as many minutes; at least he's not the only one who has trouble getting her to sit still.

They'd dropped the girls to Matt and Claire this morning before dropping Leo and Jamie uptown to hang out with friends. They've spent the day talking about Crawford and Langley and shopping.

Ben has ordered two new suits and they've looked at a new entertainment center for the living room at home – but they haven't been able to make a decision about the offer.

Ben leans over his shoulder and licks his lips.

"Waffles? Can Daddy and I come too? I love waffles."

"You can't eat my waffles though." Lucy wags her finger at him. "Daddy says you can't have syrup and chocolate and stuff like that because you might break your heart again."

"Daddy's no fun." Ben pokes his tongue at Alex.

"You can share mine, Dad. I'm going to have blueberries and bananas." Ally pops up behind her sister and Alex is relieved to see she's wearing her glasses. Her offer is met with a grimace from Ben.

"I might let you and Daddy share those. They sound… healthy. I don't think waffles are meant to be healthy."

Alex leans back against Ben, happy to listen to the girls chattering. Ally asks if Jamie and Leo will come to breakfast too; Lucy reports that Uncle Matt swears a lot when he makes cakes. Alex isn't sure if he's amused or concerned that she seems to be in awe of this. Claire finishes Lucy's hair and tells them it's time for bed.

"We'll see you in the morning. Love you." Alex blows a kiss toward the screen. Ally and Lucy crowd the camera, making fish faces and kissing sounds.

"Love you back, Daddy."

"What about me?" Ben pouts. "Do you love me too?"

More kisses follow reassurances that they love him too. Finally, they say good night and the screen goes dark. Alex sighs and tugs his hair loose of the elastic band; Ben pulls at one of the strands that springs free.

"I really am not sure how I feel about being Dad suddenly."

Alex sniggers. "Well, I suggest you get used to it because I think it's here to stay." He turns the chair around and presses his head against Ben's belly.

"You okay?"

"Yeah. Just miss them when they're not here."

"I know." Ben pulls him to his feet. "But you do realize we are completely alone for the next few hours, right? At least until the boys get home."

"So, you want to talk some more about what we're going to do?" he teases, knowing full well that's not what Ben has in mind.

"Not especially, no. I can think of more interesting ways to pass the time."

Alex sinks into the comforting warmth of Ben's arms and grins against his neck. "Uh huh."

"No kids. No teenagers. Just you, me, a bottle of wine, and a bed that hasn't seen any action in a while."

"I thought you said I was no fun?"

Ben shrugs. Presses a kiss to his forehead. "Wouldn't be the first time I was wrong."

"No kidding. Idiot."

"Hot idiot."

"Horny idiot." He nips at the skin beneath Ben's ear.

"That too. Either way, idiot who loves you."

"I love you back." Alex leans back to look at him. "Pour the wine while I get ready?"

"Deal."

The gentle glimmer of the bedside lamp sends small shadows dancing across the walls. Ben lobs his socks into the corner, followed by his shirt. Leans back against the headboard and taps the iPad screen a few times until he finds the site he wants.

Already half hard, he flicks the button on his jeans and pulls down the zipper, revealing a small patch of blue silk. Swipes his thumb over the head of his cock as he waits.

The bathroom door swings open and Alex appears, hair damp and a towel around his hips.

"Are you watching porn?" He crawls up the bed.

"No." Ben grins, tongue between his teeth, unashamed. "Maybe."

Alex chuckles and takes the glass of wine from him. Sips and peers at the screen. Scarlet stains his cheeks.

"What the… that's… nope, nope, nope. That hurts just thinking about."

"Chicken. God, you're hot when you blush." Ben plucks the glass from his hand and places it, with the iPad, on the nightstand. Opens his arms. "Come here."

Curling in against him, Alex tucks his head under his chin. Alex is four inches taller but somehow fits, and it never fails to make Ben feel strong. Protective.

"Should I be worried about not living up to a porn star?"

Ben huffs a low laugh. Runs his hand down Alex's back. "You don't have anything to worry about, trust me. You're all I need." He presses closer. "Why do you have a towel on? You should be naked."

"Because I just showered." Alex tugs at the vee of Ben's unzipped jeans. "What's your excuse?"

"I was waiting for my husband."

Ben presses his mouth to Alex's, cutting off his response. Licks along the seam of his lips until he opens them. The warm taste of wine on Alex's tongue and the low, urgent sound he makes when Ben presses him against the mattress sends desire flaming through him. He sits back on his heels, happy just to look at him. Takes his glasses off and lets them clatter onto the iPad screen.

Alex blurs, becomes softer. His chest heaves and his eyelids flutter, cock hard against his belly. He slides the tip of his tongue over his swollen bottom lip and Ben surges forward to kiss him again.

Between them, Alex's cock twitches.

"I-"

Alex reaches for him, but Ben pins his hands to the pillow either side of his head.

"Keep them there."

The order becomes an approving growl when Alex obeys, clutching at the pillow beneath his head. Driven on by his pleas and moans, Ben licks his way down his chest. A sharp nip at the coffee-colored bud of nipple makes Alex buck and whimper. Scrapes his teeth over the dip of navel. Licks his way down the line of soft hair and laps at the precum puddled on the skin beneath the head of Alex's cock.

"Ben… you… I… need... please..."

Ben loves the way he pleads, the way he uses his name still, the way he did in the early days. The way he whines and lifts his hips in a silent plea. The soft protest when he ignores him to suck at the tender spot in the crease of his thigh until a small purple bruise appears. Laves over it with his tongue. Moves to the other side and repeats the action. Back and forth he sways in a gentle rhythm, sucking and licking, as he eases himself free of his jeans and panties. Kicks them to the floor and stills for a moment, fingers curled around his own cock.

"Fuck you're hot."

Even after all their time together, he knows Alex doesn't believe it. But whenever Ben sees him like this - stretched out, panting, hard, needy - it takes every ounce of self-control to not just press into him in one smooth movement. To not lose himself in the tight heat of Alex's body; in the sound and smell and taste of his pleasure. He glances up to find Alex watching him from beneath heavy lids, teeth sunk into his lower lip.

They've been so busy - work, kids, and now this damned bombshell from Bill and Aaron - that too often things have been reduced to sleepy kisses and promises of more. Last Saturday feels a lifetime away. They *need* this - both of them.

"Turn over, baby."

Alex shivers. Does as he's asked by rolling onto his belly in a smooth, elegant movement Ben knows *he* could never emulate. He runs his hands up over the back of Alex's thighs to cup his ass cheeks. Squeezes, then spreads them. Rubs his thumbs over the creamy skin. Drags his fingers down the cleft between them and presses against the puckered muscle.

Alex moans and rubs against the bed.

"Uh-uh. No, you don't." Ben grips Alex's hips and lifts them so he's on his knees, cock bobbing and twitching.

He dips his head and sweeps his tongue over Alex's taint, up to his hole. He's rewarded with a desperate whine and a shudder. This, Ben knows, is one of Alex's favorite things. If he's relaxed enough, Ben can make him come just from this and a simple jerk of his hand.

It never fails to amuse him though that while Alex can buy him lace lingerie, and even become quite dominant - at least by Alex's standards - when Ben wears it, he still can't ask for a toy or to be rimmed without going a deep shade of purple and seeming to forget how to string words together.

Smiling at the thought - and the sight before him - Ben holds him open with both hands and circles Alex's hole with the tip of his tongue. Sucks at the delicate, pink skin until it's red and slick with spit.

Encouraged by Alex's babbles and pleas - by the thrust of his hips and the steady drip of precum - he thrusts his tongue in deeper. Rubs a finger over the area, then presses the tip in.

Keening, Alex grinds back onto it as Ben licks around the sensitive edge of muscle and skin. When he finds the spot he's looking for, he presses down until Alex cries out, rocking back harder on his tongue and finger.

Diamond-hard and aching, slick with precum, Ben's cock throbs when Alex moans.

"Ben... please... I..." Alex stammers between gasps and moans.

Ben reaches beneath him and takes him in a firm grip before closing his mouth around the spot where his finger disappears into Alex's body. As he sucks, he presses down on Alex's prostate and strokes him with swift, firm movements. A sob wracks Alex's body and his hips jerk forward.

"Oh God... Ben... I c-can't... *Ben...*"

Alex's body locks tight and he cries out as cum bursts from him, spattering onto the sheet beneath them. When Ben feels Alex's hole clamp around his finger, he presses again and sucks harder, coaxing a second smaller spurt from him. He doesn't ease up until Alex begins to loosen and soften.

Only then does he grip his own cock and rub the crown against Alex's relaxed entrance. He's too aroused for finesse; too ready to take his time. Instead, he tightens his hold and presses forward. Alex's body is relaxed enough that he's able to push in just the head of his cock, but he's already at the edge of his orgasm.

He thrusts in with a cry as it explodes from him, stealing his ability to do anything but give in to the waves of pleasure.

As the final sparks settle, he wraps his arm around Alex's waist and drags them onto their sides. Spooned together, he nuzzles at the skin beneath Alex's hair. Slides his hand between them; drags his fingers through the cum seeping from Alex's body. Grins at the sleepy protest this gets him.

"So hot," he whispers. Alex's skin is damp against his lips.

"Nope, so gross," Alex retorts, slapping his hand. "And wet. Stop."

Ben ignores him. Rubs gentle circles over the puffy skin. "I love you."

"I love you back." Alex sighs and relaxes. "You're still gross though."

Ben smiles and shuts his eyes, sated and happy.

8

Half asleep, Alex mutters under his breath as he leans across Ben's still sleeping form to grope for the phone. Finally manages to close his fingers around it and turn the damned alarm off. Why is it even set on a Sunday morning?

"Waffles," Ben mutters without opening his eyes.

"Huh?"

"Because we're meeting the girls for waffles."

Alex peers at his watch and groans. "Not for another three hours. Why do I have to be awake *now*?"

"Because I can't remember the last time that we had sex in the morning."

"You're kidding, right? Please tell me you did *not* set an alarm on a Sunday morning just so we can have sex."

Eyes still closed, Ben grins. "Beats the hell out of setting one to go for a run."

If Alex had the energy, he'd do exactly that - get up and go for a run - just to teach his husband a lesson. Instead, he rolls over and places his hand over the scar on Ben's chest; settles his head against his shoulder.

"Did you hear the boys come home last night?"

"Nope. Didn't hear anything else either."

Alex bites at Ben's ear lobe. "Don't start." He frowns. "Do you think we should check they *are* home?"

"Just because we didn't hear them getting busy doesn't mean they're not there."

"I know that you idiot, but when was the last time Leo was able to cross a room without knocking something over?"

Ben sighs. "What do I get if I go and check on two practically adult people who don't require me to check on them?"

"Go check and then you can find out."

"Baby, I'm a lawyer. I need better terms than that."

Alex sniggers. "Go and check and by the time you get back, I'm sure something will have come up that you'll be able to work with."

Ben sighs and throws back the covers.

"Put a robe on."

"But-"

"Ben!"

He smiles at the grumbling that disappears down the hallway. If Ben keeps making that much noise, he'll wake the boys up - *because of course they're home*, Alex tells himself - and that will put paid to all his Sunday morning plans.

He's slipping back toward sleep when the mattress dips and Ben slides in beside him.

"Well?"

"He's there but Leo isn't."

Alex pushes up onto his elbows. "What do you mean Leo isn't?"

"Exactly that. Kid's out for the count but he's alone. Doesn't look like Leo's been there either."

"But that doesn't make sense. Why would Leo *not* be there?"

Ben leans in and brushes his lips over Alex's. "I don't know, baby. When he wakes, we'll ask him, and I promise to not tease him about anything. But right now? I was promised a reward for getting out of bed so early-"

"You're the one who set the alarm!"

"Yes, but I had no intention of leaving the bed. So if it's okay with you – less chatty, more sexy."

Alex raises one eyebrow. "This is what passes for romantic now? Less chatty, more sexy?"

"It does when time is limited."

Ben kisses him again and Alex decides that he may have a point.

9

Ben sips his coffee and watches the couple at the table next to them. Dad bounces a baby on his knee while Mom helps a toddler wearing Mickey Mouse ears to eat a forkful of pancake.

He glances toward the corner of the coffee shop where Lucy, wearing her own set of ears, is exploring a large plastic chest of toys. Ally, cross-legged next to her, reads *Matilda*. Twists and untwists a strand of hair around her fingers. He smiles and looks back at the couple with the baby and toddler. Sighing, he reaches for the last morsel of waffle on his plate. He catches Alex watching him and shrugs.

"Everything okay?" Matt looks from Ben to Alex and back.

Alex grins. "Someone thinks he'd like to have a baby in the house again."

"Seriously?" Jamie, who has been quiet all morning, looks startled. They'd tried asking him about Leo, but he'd simply said he'd gone back to the dorm and changed the subject.

"Don't look at me." Claire holds her hands up in mock defense. "You guys are great parents and all that and I love you but two is my limit."

Beneath the table, Ben rubs Alex's ankle with his foot. "Everybody calm down." He nods when the waitress offers him more coffee. "We're just talking about it. No decisions yet about…" he glances at Alex, "anything."

"What about a goldfish?" Matt suggests. "Be cheaper and easier to care for. No college to pay for either." He lifts his chin toward Jamie. "Speaking of which, you headed this way in the fall, kiddo?"

Jamie ducks his head. Picks up his fork and pushes what Ben now sees is his uneaten waffle around the plate. "I'm…" he takes a deep breath, "actually, no. I'm not going to UCLA."

Ben's bangs his coffee cup down. "What do you mean you're not going to UCLA?"

Alex swivels in his seat, mouth hanging open. "Jamie?"

"I was going to tell you tonight; I think I want to go somewhere else. Or maybe take a gap year."

"I beg your pardon?" Ben's confused. "I thought you were set on coming up here to be with Leo?"

Jamie's lower lip trembles when he looks up. "We broke up."

"What? When?" The words come out louder than Ben had intended. The couple at the next table glance over, concern etched on their faces. Ally and Lucy stop what they're doing to watch them. Ally's glasses don't hide her worry. He smiles, hoping to reassure her and turns his attention back to Jamie.

"Why didn't you say something earlier?" He narrows his eyes. "Did he do something? Did he hit you?"

"Ben, shhh." Alex pulls his chair closer to Jamie's. "Do you want to talk about it?"

"Nothing to talk about." The shine in Jamie's eyes suggests that might not be quite true. "We broke up is all. Happens every day, right?"

"That's not the point." Alex rubs his shoulder. "What happened?"

"Can we *not* talk about it right now?" Jamie looks around the table. "I don't want to spoil Disney for the girls."

Ben scowls. "Okay, but buddy, you can't not go to college just because you broke up with your boyfriend."

"Ben!" Annoyance flashes in Alex's hazel eyes. "Not now!"

Before Ben can protest the scolding, Jamie pushes his chair back and stands. Instead of the tantrum Ben expects, he sounds sad and tired.

"Dad, I didn't say I wasn't going to college. I said I wasn't going to UCLA." He steps away from the table. "And for the record - that's *why* he dumped me. Because I told him I want to go somewhere else. I'm going to wait outside, okay?"

Astounded, Ben watches him walk away. A slap on the back of his hand drags his attention back to Alex, who glares at him.

"Maybe next time, let the kid breathe before you jump down his throat?"

"What? I didn't jump down his throat. I was just trying to be practical."

"He doesn't need practical, Ben. He needs comfort."

Through the window, Ben spots Jamie sitting on one of the benches in front of the cafe. Head bowed, shoulders drooping, Ben hasn't seen him look this dejected since he came to live with them. He sighs.

"I know, I know, I'm an idiot. I'll go talk to him."

The spring breeze wraps around him when he steps outside, and he regrets not having grabbed his jacket. Jamie is hunched over, arms around himself. Ben sits next to him and, ignoring the passers-by, slips his arm around the boy's shoulders.

"Want to tell me what happened?"

Jamie slumps against him. "He says that if I'm not coming up to the city there isn't any point carrying on 'cause long distance doesn't work'." He sniffles and scrubs at his face with the back of his hand. "That he has all these offers and that if I'm not going to be here, he might as well take advantage of them."

Ben winces. That has to hurt, even if it does sound to his ears like a ploy to make Jamie jealous.

"He went back to the dorm with some guys before the show ended."

"And he just left you there? Alone?" A rush of anger fills Ben. "Why didn't you phone us? We would have come and picked you up."

"I was okay; you and Dad were having a date night. I called an Uber."

"Not the point. I know you're not a little kid anymore, but this isn't San Cap."

Jamie nods against Ben's chest. "Doesn't matter anymore anyway." He sits up and offers Ben a watery smile. "The others are coming. Can we talk about the rest of it later?"

Ben sighs. "Yeah, of course. We'll talk about school when we get home, but for what it's worth though, kiddo, Leo is way out of line."

Jamie considers this a moment. Shrugs. "Maybe. I dunno. I just -"

Lucy cuts his words off as she flings herself against him. She wraps her arms around his legs and looks up. "Jamie, will you take me on the teacups? Will you? Daddy says his tummy can't cope with one more spinny thing and Papa already did them twice. Please, please, please, please."

Jamie bends and lifts her up. It occurs to Ben that she's too tall for it to be even remotely comfortable with his slender frame.

"You sure you don't want to go on the roller coaster?"

Lucy's eyes widen. "I do, but Daddy says I'm too little, and that's not even true because I'm not little. I'm big."

"And?" Alex whispers in Ben's ear.

"I'll tell you while they're on the spinny thing."

10

Alex twists around to check on the girls in the back seat. Both are sound asleep under the latest addition to their ever-growing collection of Disney blankets, each clutching new toys.

"We're never going to get them to sleep when we get home, you realize."

Ben pats his knee. "You say that every time. They'll be fine."

As usual, they'd left Disneyland later than intended. It doesn't seem to matter what they do; it always happens. Normally, he insists they go on the Saturday but this time around it just hadn't worked well with Matt and Claire. Now, the girls will sleep until they get home, then resist any and all attempts to get them bathed and into bed. Tomorrow morning will be just as much fun, and nobody will want to get up on time. Himself included.

Fine. Right.

Late nights and Monday mornings aside, they still have the issue of the *Crawford and Langley* offer to deal with; not to mention… he looks over his shoulder at Jamie. Huddled against the door, unplugged headphones hanging around his neck, he has Ally's glasses in a loose grip. Holds them out when he notices Alex looking at him.

"Didn't want them to fall off and get broken."

Alex takes them and tucks them in his pocket. "You okay?"

"No."

He sounds so young and sad; it tugs at Alex's heart. Poor kid. He wishes he knew how to help.

"What made you decide not to go to UCLA?"

Seemingly surprised by the question, Jamie's eyes flick to Ben then back to Alex. "I don't know. USC just has a really good art department and I can do the first two years at the satellite campus in San Cap." He looks out the window. "Besides, you go there."

Alex frowns. "I don't understand."

"Lots of the kids in my class are going to the same college as their folks."

Alex considers this answer for a moment. Ben, he can tell, is paying close attention to the conversation, casting the occasional look in the rear-view mirror.

"Dad went to UCLA," Alex points out.

"Yeah, I know, but he went to law school and I don't want to be a lawyer."

That statement usually results in good natured teasing from Ben but this time he's silent. Jamie nibbles at his thumbnail and avoids looking at either of them, but especially Ben.

Alex stretches back to nudge his hand away from his mouth.

"Also, I -" Jamie hesitates, "I've only just found you guys. I don't think I want to move away yet."

Touched, Alex straightens in his seat to mull this new information over. He flicks a glance at Ben but says nothing.

"And that's why Leo's upset?" Ben asks. He's still watching the road, but Alex isn't fooled. When Ben had recounted what had happened, he'd been furious that Leo had abandoned Jamie at the concert the night before.

Jamie's laugh holds no humor. A cynical sound that shakes Alex even more than the sadness had. "Upset. Yeah, let's call it that."

"He's -" Alex begins, but Jamie cuts him off.

"He's gonna see other people even though I told him it wouldn't change anything. Me staying in San Cap, I mean. I could drive up at weekends or he could come down." His voice breaks and Alex reaches back to touch his hand. "He just said something about long distance not working and left with the guys from his dorm."

Ben mumbles something that Alex doesn't quite hear but sounds a lot like "gonna kick the little shit's ass".

"Probably better, anyway," Jamie continues, "better to get it out of the way now than move up there and have him dump me anyway, right?"

"I'm so sorry." The words sound lame, but what else can he say? The thought that they might actually have a solution to the problem doesn't help. "Maybe if you give it some time, he'll come around."

Jamie swipes his arm across his eyes. "Whatever."

Hoping to steer the conversation to less painful territory, Alex pulls the university website up on his phone. "Have you thought about what subjects you'd like to do - wherever you decide to go?"

Jamie shrugs. "Not really."

Alex looks at Ben and sees his own disbelief reflected on his face. Knowing Jamie, if he's decided on the college already, he has a fair idea of the courses he wants to take. He's trying to decide how to point this out without making Jamie defensive when Ally sits up and rubs her eyes. Yawns.

"Daddy, are we nearly home?" Before Alex can answer, she frowns and peers down her nose. "Where are my glasses?"

He pulls them from his pocket and gives them to her.

The strident shrill of Ben's cell phone ringing fills the car. On the dash, the Bluetooth screen displays FIONA. Ben taps the button on the steering wheel to connect the call.

"Hey Fiona, what's up?"

"Ben, where are you?" Her voice, through the speakers, is shaky. As if she's been crying. Alex frowns, Jamie's college choices forgotten.

"Daddy?" Lucy lifts her head, still mostly asleep. Alex holds his finger to his lips.

"About thirty minutes out of San Cap," Ben replies, "why?"

Dread, thick and sour, clogs Alex's throat and chest when she doesn't answer immediately.

"Ben." Fiona's voice cracks. To Alex's horror, he realizes she *is* crying and knows with sharp, cutting certainty he doesn't want to hear whatever she is about to say. "Your house is on fire."

11

Ben tightens his grip on the steering wheel. *What* did Fiona just say? He had to have misheard her. He would have sworn she said the house was on fire. That can't possibly be… he looks at Alex and the truth hits him.

He slams both feet onto the brake pedal. Curses as the car fishtails to the side of the road.

"Papa?" Ally whimpers. Jamie whispers, "come here babe" and he hears the sound of her seat belt being unbuckled.

"Ben?" Fiona's voice seems distant, as if she's at the end of a very long tunnel.

So close.

So damned far.

"How bad?"

"Ben, I-"

"How bad?" He bites the words out, knuckles going white with the force of his grip on the wheel.

"The firemen are doing everything they can, but it's not looking good."

Everything feels distorted and somehow removed, as if it's happening somewhere just out of reach. Alex's hand on his bicep. Lucy mumbling in the back seat. The thump of Dork Dog's tail against the rear window.

"Ben?"

It's the fear in Alex's voice that cuts through the fog. He stomps the gas pedal to the floor and pretends he doesn't hear his gasp or Jamie's hushed reassurances to Ally as he buckles her seat belt once more.

"We'll be there in fifteen minutes." Without waiting for a reply, he disconnects the call and starts replaying Fiona's words in his head. The house is burning. Firemen are there. Doing everything they can. But…

"Ben!"

Alex's voice is sharp rather than loud. Ben tears his gaze from the road in front of them. "*What?*"

"You need to slow down."

He flicks his eyes at the road and then back to Alex. "The …"

"The kids are in the back."

The words are quiet. Anybody else might even have found them calm. But the tone does for Ben what the actual words can't. It calms the roaring panic in his head.

The needle hovers at one hundred.

He eases his foot back.

Alex squeezes his knee, and it's the first that Ben notices his hand is even there. "Thank you."

"I notified the alarm service that we were out of town. That's why they called Fiona." He's not sure why he's telling Alex something he already knows, except somehow it helps keep the fear from cartwheeling out of control. "They were supposed to come tomorrow and add extra cameras and a sprinkler system."

He knows why he's telling Alex *that*. In the wake of the last three fires, the alarm companies in San Cap have been inundated with orders. Tomorrow had been the earliest day they could get there. He wishes he'd insisted on Friday.

Alex gives his knee another light squeeze and shakes his head. "Sweetheart, don't." As if he's read his mind. "It's not your fault."

Easy for Alex to say; not so easy for Ben to believe.

***

At the entrance to the street, a roadblock forces him to stop the car. A young, uniformed police officer he recognizes but whose name he can't remember approaches and Ben gets out of the car. Stumbles when he breathes in the smoke-filled air.

That's my home I can smell, he thinks as he yanks open Lucy's door.

"I'm sorry Sir - oh Mister Larsen, it's you. I'm afraid you can't stop ther -"

"Buddy," Ben interrupts, "that's my fucking house that's burning. I'll stop wherever the hell I want. Keep an eye on my dog."

On the other side of the car, Ally in his arms, Alex sighs. "Ben."

Ben swallows his impatience. "Sorry. Please, keep an eye on my dog."

"I understand, Mister Larsen, but I really can't let -"

"Nobody's asking you to let me do anything."

Ben pushes past him, pressing Lucy's head into his neck to try and keep her from breathing in too much smoke. A hand on his elbow stops him and he turns, ready to do battle with the cop again. Instead, he sees Alex, still carrying Ally. Behind him is Jamie, eyes huge with panic.

Alex simply nods and together, they push through the crowd that has gathered. A few people - neighbors - recognize them and move away murmuring words of sympathy and support.

As they come around the corner, Ben stops and stares. Shock steals his breath. In his arms Lucy whimpers and squirms but he refuses to let her down.

Red and orange flames reach for the night sky. Droplets of water fly from the fire hoses, reflecting and magnifying the brightness tenfold. Steam and smoke billow together to turn the air thick and heavy.

The roof above their bedroom collapses bringing memories crashing over him as he watches: doing his homework in there as a teenager, coaxing Alex out of his pajamas during his first visit, dozing in the armchair with the girls as babies in his arms, Dork Dog in his basket in the corner.

"Ben!"

He snaps around at the sound of Alex's voice. Face smeared with cinders, sweat - or maybe tears, Ben can't tell - Alex's eyes are red-rimmed and shocked.

Ally sobs against his shoulder.

Jamie seems unaware that he's chewing his left thumbnail as he stares at the scene before them; blood trickles down the digit.

Lucy digs her fingers into his neck, her breath coming in harsh gasps against his skin.

What the hell is he thinking?

They shouldn't be here; shouldn't be seeing this. He reaches out and gently eases Jamie's thumb from his mouth before winding his arm around Alex's waist and directing him back the way they've come.

"Ben! Alex!" Fiona shoulders her way through the crowd. She throws her arms around him and Lucy. "Oh, thank God I found you. They weren't going to let me through. Ernie Danes is over here, waiting for you."

She leads them toward a group of men gathered around the open door of a truck. *San Capistrano Fire Department* is written on the glossy paint of the vehicle. A large, solid man in an open-throated shirt straightens when they get near and holds his hand out toward Ben.

"Ben. I'm so sorry, kid." Ernie Danes, Fire Chief for nearly twenty years, had dated Allie briefly when Ben was in his early twenties. Their split had been a mutual decision, and they'd remained friends. He'd spoken at Allie's funeral and when Ben and Alex had moved back to San Capistrano after Ally's birth, had gone out of his way to welcome them.

"Do we know if it's the same as the others?" He's pretty sure he knows the answer.

"Not for sure but I'd say it's a safe bet."

Ben nods. A safe bet. Yeah.

Fiona tries to take Lucy from him and gets a silent glare of refusal for her trouble. He gives her a sad smile and hefts Lucy into a more comfortable position. Danes continues.

"Do you have somewhere you can take your family? We're doing everything we can here; you need to take care of your kids."

Bewildered, Ben stares at him. Take his family somewhere? Where? Back to Los Angeles? To the apartment? To Matt and Claire's? No; that won't work. Fiona clears her throat.

"I've booked a suite at The Regency for you." She looks around the group. "They've said it's okay to take Bart with you."

Bart. Fuck! Dork Dog is still in the car, with the young cop looking after him. *If* the young cop is still looking after him. God, he hopes he's okay.

"Good. The Regency is good." Danes strokes his finger down Lucy's cheek. "Go there and I'll be in touch as soon as I can." Ben opens his mouth, but Danes nudges him away. "Go on. There's nothing you can do here."

12

Alex turns out the bathroom light and goes into the living room. Ally and Lucy, in new pajamas Claire and Matt had bought them yesterday, are stretched out in front of the television watching cartoons. Shock has already painted purple shadows beneath their eyes and left their faces pale.

Curled up in an oversized armchair, head bent over his phone and a fresh Band-Aid on his left thumb, Jamie taps at the screen. Alex wonders if he's texting Leo. He rakes his fingers through his damp but at least smoke-free hair and sits down. Immediately the girls clamber onto his lap.

"Daddy." Ally's eyes fill with tears. "Our house."

"Are all our toys burned up? And our clothes?" Lucy asks. "Do we live here now?"

He tucks a curl of hair behind her ear. Avoids the first two questions by answering the third. "No, honey, we don't live here now. We're just going to stay here for a little while."

"How long?"

"I don't know. While Papa and I…" The words trail off. While he and Ben what? Find somewhere to live? Buy them new clothes? New toys? What does he tell them? All they have left is in the few bags in the suite and Alex's car. Jamie looks up from his phone. Alex opts for the only thing he can think of to say. "While Papa and I figure it out."

"Will Papa be back from walking Bart soon?" Ally rests her head on his shoulder.

"Soon." Alex hopes he's right; Ben should have been back by now. Hopefully, he hasn't taken it into his stubborn head to go back to… to go back there.

"I'm hungry." As if to underline her words, Lucy's tummy gives a loud gurgle. She giggles and claps her hands over the source of the sound.

"Me too." Jamie shoves his phone in his pocket. Stretches.

"What about you, Monster?" Alex tilts his head to watch Ally's face. She gives him a somber look.

"What about Papa?"

It's not lost on Alex that she's reverted to Papa and Daddy.

As if on cue, the door swings open and Bart trots in followed by Ben carrying two large pizzas and a paper bag. The smell of hot, melted cheese chases the lingering smell of smoke from Alex's nose and reminds him that he's hungry too.

"Pizza! Yay!" Lucy jumps around in a circle, clapping her hands.

Alex stands and goes to Ben. Taking the pizzas and bag, he kisses Ben.

"Go wash up," he murmurs before turning back to Lucy. "Okay, everyone needs to go with Papa and wash their hands, then come to the table. Quietly."

"But we just had a bath," Lucy protests.

"You also just hugged Bart. Hands."

He places the pizzas on the table and flips back the lids. One has ham, cheese, and mushrooms - the girls' and Jamie's favorite. The other has olives, pepperoni, and one half is covered with capers even though Ben hates them. Exhausted, Alex picks one off and pops it in his mouth.

***

Lucy is asleep before Alex leaves the room and despite a fresh burst of tears still drying on her cheeks, Ally is fading fast. In the living room, Jamie is once more in the armchair in the corner, this time with his laptop balanced on his lap. At the table, Ben lines up three tumblers and pulls a bottle of whiskey from the paper bag. He splashes a hefty amount into two of the glasses and offers one to Alex. Pours soda for Jamie.

"Hey, kiddo." When Jamie looks up, Ben holds his glass out to him.

Alex sits on the sofa and takes a sip from his own glass; the alcohol is smooth and rich on his tongue. Setting his laptop on the floor, Jamie scoots closer and takes the glass being offered to him.

Sinking down next to him, Ben sighs, takes his glasses off and tosses them on the coffee table and when Alex looks in his eyes, he recognizes the glassy sheen of shock. He puts his drink on the table, then takes the tumbler from Ben's hand, and places it next to his.

He curls his fingers around Ben's wrist; counts his pulse with practiced ease. Satisfied his heart is okay for now, Alex rests their heads together. Suppresses a shudder at the smell of smoke in Ben's hair.

"It's okay, sweetheart."

Jamie kneels on the floor at Ben's feet and leans against his thigh. When Ben reaches out to stroke his hair, his hand shakes. Alex braces himself.

"When I…" Ben's voice falters; he licks his lips and starts again. "When I was a little kid - about Ally's age, maybe a bit younger - my mom worked for an architectural firm over in Burswood and we lived in this bungalow near the high school. She would work all day and then at night while Polly and I watched television she would design her own stuff. She had this really old drafting desk and she'd make tea and she'd just sit and draw these houses." He gulps his whiskey. "Some of them went on to win awards. She was good. *Really* good."

Alex hugs him. "Yeah, she was."

He picks up his own drink and sips.

"Every Sunday though she'd make herself a Gibson, get out this one design and she'd tinker with it. Add things here, remove stuff there. Tweak the layout. And she'd talk about how she was going to build it one day and we'd live in it. There would be room for Polly to write her books and space for me to have my bike and maybe a dog one day." A tear slides down his cheek and falls to the back of his hand. "She said she'd have her own studio and clients." His teeth chatter when he pauses; Alex pulls the throw from the back of the sofa around him. Rubs his back to try and warm him. "I was eleven when she won her first big award and started really earning good money. About a year later, she took Polly and me out to see this empty lot by the beach. New neighborhood, good area. A month later they broke ground on the place."

"Do you remember the first time you took me home to meet her and Polly?" Alex asks. "I was just blown away by the house. I thought it should have been on a magazine cover and you said it had been."

"Yeah." Ben takes another mouthful of whiskey; stares into space, gaze seemingly fixed on nothing. "You didn't want to have sex because it was my mother's house."

Blushing, Alex offers an apologetic grin to Jamie, who returns it with a shrug.

"You said," Alex continues, "that the house put you through law school, but I never did find out what you meant."

Sadness steals some of the shine from Ben's smile. "It won House of the Year, and Mom was all over the architectural and design magazines as the one to watch. In less than a year, she was turning clients away, she was so busy. Between her and Polly…" He takes a shaky breath. "My mom's house is gone."

"Papa…" Jamie touches his hand.

As Alex watches, the shock recedes from Ben's eyes and gives way to grief as he seems to grasp - truly grasp - what has happened. A shudder wracks his body from somewhere deep within him, and pain floods his face.

"My mom's house is gone." His voice is little more than a rasp. He collapses against Alex. "My mom's house is gone," he repeats. Alex tightens his hold as his shoulders hitch and a sob tears from him. "It's gone… *she's* gone."

Unable to speak for the lump in his throat, Alex pulls him closer. From his first visit, the beach house has been home for him and each time his thoughts sidle up to the loss, panic cramps his stomach and closes his throat.

How must Ben, who grew up there, feel?

He rests his cheek against Ben's sweat-spiked hair and searches for something – anything - to reassure him. In the end he says nothing; he simply holds him tighter and lets him cry.

13

They'd finally fallen asleep in the early hours of the morning, only to be woken around five by Ally climbing into the bed between the two of them, shivering and crying. She'd eventually settled and gone back to sleep, leaving the two of them to doze on and off until seven-thirty.

After showering, they'd taken the kids downstairs for breakfast, where Ben had soon grown tired of the well-meant sympathy from the staff. He doesn't want sympathy; he wants his house.

Fiona, looking as tired as he feels, had arrived as they finished up and had taken the kids into the village to get toiletries and some groceries for the room. It had taken some coaxing, but Ally had finally gone, clinging to Jamie's hand and looking back over her shoulder until Ben had had to turn away.

Matt and Claire are somewhere between here and the city and will meet them back at the hotel.

And now he and Alex are here.

The stench of smoke and wet ash is heavy in the early morning air, making his stomach roil and churn.

Ben is surprised by the number of people still milling around what is left of the house the next morning. To the right sit the charred hulks of the cars, surrounded by smoldering remnants of the garage. Close to the beach is a single wall - black and crumbling around a gaping hole that had once housed the impressive stained-glass feature window. It takes him a few minutes to realize that the splashes of color he sees on the ground around it, are shards of the window itself. Little else of his office is recognizable; everything has melted and fused together.

Light ribbons of smoke - or perhaps steam - rise from the now sooty cobbles of the courtyard. The table where they'd welcomed Jamie, the girls' trampoline, the loungers where he'd told Alex he loved him the first time and where once they had made love in the moonlight - nothing remains.

Everything is gone.

Finally, he makes himself look at the house. At what is left of it. Some of the downstairs framework still stands. A misshapen mound that he thinks may have been their lounge suite. Weirdly, the kitchen island where they'd prepared meals and cocktails seems to be more or less intact. Like everything else it is darkened by ash and soot but seems to be otherwise unscathed. Ben can't help snorting.

"You were right, Mom. Marble lasts forever. Should have built the whole fucking place in it."

Alex raises an eyebrow, and Ben shakes his head. It won't make sense to anybody but him and right now, he doesn't think he can explain it. Nearby, Danes points out something to a member of his team; he returns Ben's raised hand with a nod.

Slumping against the hood of Alex's car, Ben scrubs at the stubble on his chin. Adjusts his glasses. The car dips a little when Alex joins him.

"Ben?"

"What a fucking mess."

Alex takes his hand and squeezes it, lifting his chin in the direction of the house. *Remains of the house*, Ben corrects in his head.

Danes approaches; fatigue carves lines into his face and circles of sweat stain his shirt. He shakes Ben's hand.

"I'd ask how you're doing today, but I can imagine. How are the kids holding up?"

Alex rocks his hand back and forth in the air in a 'so-so' gesture.

"I'm so sorry, guys." Danes claps Ben on the shoulder and for a moment they stare at the rubble in silence. The older man clears his throat. "We did everything we could, I swear." He looks at Ben. "It was an amazing house, Ben. I wish we'd been able to save it for you."

"You did your best, Ernie. I know that and I'm grateful." He kicks a pebble; it sends up a tiny cloud of ash when it lands. "Last night, you said you thought it was a safe bet it was the same guy as the others. Care to expand yet?"

Danes looks miserable and Ben doesn't blame him one bit. If they're right, this is the fourth fire in five weeks and they're no closer to catching whoever is behind them.

"What can I say? Same type of fire, same set-up, all used the same accelerant – so yeah, we're confident it's the same son of a bitch. The good thing – if you can call it that - is he always makes sure nobody's home, so people aren't his direct targets at least."

"Thank God for that." Alex tugs on the hem of Ben's shirt, his face pale and sad.

Ben reaches out and pulls him a little closer. Takes comfort in the warm, solid familiarity of his body. Staring at the debris, he knows he needs to ask what they have to do next but can't bring himself to form the words. Instead, he opts for what he little he knows.

"Our alarm company might have some video from last night. I don't know if you'll be able to get anything off it but who knows?"

"Hey, it's definitely worth a look. And obviously we're going to have to sit down and go over things officially, so after I've spoken to your guys, I'll give you a call."

"Thanks. I have to head to the courthouse next to ask for a continuance in my case, but we'll be back at The Regency this afternoon. We'll be based there for the next few days while we…" he takes a breath and forces himself to continue, "until we figure something out." He digs in his pocket for his wallet and takes out a business card. "This is my number, and obviously, you can always talk to Alex."

From the corner of his eye, Ben sees Alex walking toward what remains of the garage. Ben shakes hands with Danes and follows him.

The line of still smoking metal skeletons reminds Ben of the pictures he's seen of whale carcasses. The old Volvo that had been Allie's, then Alex's, and finally Jamie's, is a hulking black skeleton beside his sedan, and at the end, his beloved Targus. This last pierces his resolve to remain calm, stopping him in his steps. The car had belonged to his grandfather, and Polly had given it to him when he'd graduated from law school.

He'd driven Alex down here from the city in it the first time he'd brought him to meet Allie and Polly. He can't believe it's gone.

Everything is gone.

Without a word, he turns and walks back along the cobbles that had edged this side of the house. Follows them around what would have been the outside of Jamie's room, the kitchen, the laundry. Walks through the destruction that now makes up their courtyard and down to the beach.

Here, nothing has changed. Still the same distance to the damp sand showing where the tide has been. The same gentle wind lifting the tails of his shirt. The same gentle splash of water on land. The familiar crunch of scattered shells beneath his feet. Gulls circle and scream overhead.

Panting, he stares out at the water.

"Sweetheart?" Alex slides his arms around his waist.

"I was fine until I saw the cars." He blows a breath out through his nose. "Well maybe not fine, but I was okay."

"Yeah, I know." Alex tightens his hold. "When I saw the Volvo, all I could think was that we don't need to get Roger to look at it now."

Ben huffs; the sound sad and dejected. "Aint that the truth? I just can't believe it's all..."

His voice dies away.

"Ben, it..."

Emotion rushes him, thick and cloying as the smoke last night. He shifts out of Alex's embrace. Throws his hands in the air, grief distorting his face.

"Look I *know* it's all just… *stuff.* I *know* the important thing is that nobody was home and that you and the kids and Bart are all safe, it's just… it's my home. It's all I had left of my mother and my grandmother and it's gone." He clenches and unclenches his fists by his sides as if it will help him grasp the words. "I feel like… like…"

"Like we lost them all over again?" Alex asks gently.

On the list of the things Ben loves about his husband, his ability to know what he's feeling – and to understand it - is near the top. Right next to the gentleness of his touch when he pulls Ben back into his arms.

Neither of them moves as the water laps at their feet.

14

"Daddy?"

Alex drops the screwdriver he's using, glares at the unfinished bookcase, and turns to Ally. She leans against the doorjamb, tugging on the end of her ponytail.

"What's up, monster?"

"Is this our home now?"

He sighs.

Before the end of a week of hotel living, they had all been out of sorts. Lucy seemed to have decided that the only possible way she could cope was by annoying both of her siblings as much as possible. Even taking them to the beach with Bart twice a day hadn't helped.

Bill Langley had called to tell Ben that if they needed anything at all, the firm would be more than happy to help. That while they understood that it was the last thing he needed to worry about right now, the offer was still on the table.

After stepping in to break up what had felt like the millionth squabble between the girls only to hear Jamie yell "Dad, tell Lucy to knock it the f – hell off" ten minutes later, Alex had finally conceded defeat. Ignoring the ruckus from the other end of the suite, he'd gone to the bedroom where Ben had been trying to answer emails and insisted on two things. The kids needed to go back to school, and they *had* to find somewhere to live.

Two days later, with help from Fiona and their realtor, they'd made an offer on this place. Four bedrooms, two bathrooms, and a fenced yard for Bart. It's not perfect, but it will give them enough space to get through the next few months without going crazy. They can make it work.

He hopes.

It had belonged to a family from Los Angeles who'd kept it as a holiday home and was empty. When they'd heard about the fire, they'd been happy to let them move in immediately. He and Ben had then spent a day buying furniture, appliances, and God knows what else and arranging for delivery.

This morning Claire and Fiona had dropped the kids off at school – even Jamie had been happy to go back - while Alex, Ben, and Matt had come here to wait for everything to arrive.

They've spent the afternoon trying to set up televisions and assemble bookcases and make the place feel like home.

Alex pats the carpet and waits for her to come in and sit down, cross legged, next to him. Her shoelace is untied and there's a smudge of something on her cheek. Alex tries to rub it away, smiling when she pushes his hand away.

"Yeah baby girl. This is our new house for now."

"I want our house back."

He puts his arm around her and rests his cheek on her head. "I know. We all do, sweetheart."

"Logan at school says that our house got burned down because of you and Papa."

He frowns, trying to place Logan in his mind.

"Who's Logan?"

"He's a big boy at school. He's in Miss Donaldson's class. He said it's because you and Papa are…" She falters, clearly unsure of the words she wants.

"Because Papa and I are gay?" Alex forces himself to keep his tone light but his stomach clenches. There's never been a problem with the school before. Granted, he and Ben aren't the only same gender parents in town and with their jobs, they're fairly well known, but he doesn't think it's just that. San Cap is a liberal, caring community – it's why they love living here.

He hopes that's not changing.

Ally nods. "Yeah. Only he didn't say gay. He used a bad word, and he said it's not normal and that we should have a mommy." She scrubs at her nose with the back of her hand.

Bile, hot and acidic, rises in his throat and he swallows it back.

"And what did you say to Logan?"

Ally bows her head and picks at the loose shoelace.

"Ally?"

"I - I told him he was an a-hole." She turns to look at him, eyes flashing behind her glasses. "I know it's a bad word, but he used one first and he was mean, and he was wrong." She glares at him. "And dumb."

He pulls her into a hug.

"You're right, he *was* being mean, and he *was* wrong, but you shouldn't call people dumb."

Ally tilts her head back and peers up at him, eyes narrowed. In that moment she looks so much like Ben it takes Alex's breath away. The flash of mischief in her eyes is all Ben too, and Alex taps the tip of her nose with his finger.

"And I'd rather you didn't call him an a-hole either." Even if he is one, he thinks but doesn't add.

"But –"

Alex raises his eyebrows but says nothing.

"Okay." The word is heavy with reluctance. "But I don't think it's fair -"

"It's *not* fair, but Daddy's right."

Alex jumps at the sound of Ben's voice. When did he get there?

Ben comes into the bedroom and crouches in front of them.

"The person who burned down our house did it because they like to burn down houses, that's all. They burned down other people's homes too, remember, and the police are doing everything they can to catch them, so they don't do it to anybody else." He tips her head back with the tip of his finger. "Daddy and I will go and see your teacher and talk to her about Logan, okay?"

"Okay."

"So no more bad words, got it?"

Pushing her glasses back into place, she gives them an unenthusiastic nod that leaves Alex certain they'll be revisiting that particular subject in the not-too-distant future.

Ben grins at her. "That's my girl. On Monday, while you're at school, I have to go up to the city. How about I call into the apartment and pick up some of your toys from up there?"

Her eyes light up. "Yes, yes, yes. Can I have my Elsa and my Anna dolls? And my Olaf! Oh, and my books that are there?"

Alex chuckles. "Why don't you go and make a list for Papa to take with him?"

She runs from the room, ignoring Alex's plea for her to tie her laces up before she trips. The last thing they need is a split lip or sprained ankle.

"When did you turn into a grown-up?" He turns his face up to Ben and accepts a kiss.

Ben shrugs. "When our daughter started having to deal with homophobic bullshit at school."

"Yeah, well don't forget that he's just a kid, and he's only parroting what he's heard from the adults around him." Alex picks up the screwdriver and studies the bookcase again. He still has to put together Lucy's one and one for the living room. There's no point asking Ben – it had taken him three hours to put a new television cabinet together, only to find he'd put half of the panels on back to front.

Ben kisses him again. "You're a good man, Alex Davis."

"Mmmhmmm, that's why you love me. Going up to talk to Langley?"

"Yeah. I know they said we can take our time, but I'd like to ask them a few questions and I thought I'd call in and see the insurance guys at the same time. Stop at the apartment for some stuff."

Bridging finance for the house hadn't been a problem for which they're both grateful, but it's added to the pressure to make a decision about the deal. Accepting the offer would make waiting for the insurance settlement less stressful, but Alex suspects that Ben is concerned about how Crawford and Langley see the merger now.

"Want me to come with you?"

Ben shakes his head. "No. I doubt I can be back before school's out and the kids need you. Are you going to go to work?"

"Yeah and I'll try to make it to my morning class too but that depends on the level of chaos here." He's not hopeful about that at all; chaos is what his family is best at.

Ben kisses him. "Why don't you leave that bookcase for now and come have a drink."

"No, I want to finish it so I can do Lucy's before dinner."

"I told you we should have bought them already assembled." Ben rolls his sleeves up. "Okay, what do you need me to do?"

15

Sighing, Ben stretches out on the new couch. Why did they never get a longer sofa before? Both he and Alex are over six feet, they have children and a Dork Dog – this thing is long overdue. Refusing to think about *why* they need the new couch, he covers his eyes with his arm and lets his mind drift.

"He's adorable." Allie links her arm through his. He holds his other arm out for Polly to do the same. The sound of the water against the sand is soothing. Familiar. "I hope we'll be seeing more of him."

"You will." He can't help smiling at the thought of the man inside packing their bags. "I love him."

"Oh, we know." Polly smirks. "You, child, really do have to work on using your inside voice." She pauses before adding, "so to speak."

Ben groans and shakes his head. "Don't you dare say anything like that to Alex. He'll never speak to me again."

Patting his arm, Allie smiles. "I don't think you have too much to worry about in that department, honey. He seems as smitten with you as you are with him."

"Smitten, huh?"

"You two are so cute, it's kind of nauseating." She looks up at him. "Have you told him how you feel?"

He nods, aware of the blush pricking at his skin.

"And what did he say to that?" Polly asks, eyes glimmering with amusement.

"That he loves me back."

The knowledge fills Ben with a warmth he's never felt before, cocooning him in something he's unable to describe. Something huge and breath-taking and overwhelming.

"In that case," Polly says, "you must take good care of him, child. He's a good man."

"Yes. Yes, he is." He hugs the two women closer.

They turn toward the house. Ben can see Alex in the kitchen window; he looks as if he belongs there. As if the window has just been waiting for him to arrive.

If someone was to ask Ben why he's smiling, he would answer "because this is what I think heaven is." This house, this courtyard, the sound of the sea behind him, his mother and grandmother – and waiting inside for him, Alex.

Yes, this is what heaven would be.

"Ben? Are you okay?"

Ben lifts his arm and is met with a worried hazel gaze. Alex brushes his thumb over his cheek and it's only then that Ben realizes he's crying.

He sits up and scrubs at his face. "Yeah. I'm fine. I… uh… I was remembering the first time I brought you down here to meet Mom and Polly. The day after Polly's birthday and we were getting ready to go home. I was out on the sand with them and you were packing our stuff."

"I remember." Alex sits next to him and takes his hand. "I double checked every bag for spiders."

Chuckling, Ben nods. "I told them that I loved you and when I looked up, I saw you in the kitchen and I remember I thought you looked like you belonged there."

His voice breaks.

Alex squeezes his hand and tears fill his eyes. "Ben…"

Before he can add anything more, the doorbell rings. Bart leaps up and rushes toward the door, tail wagging.

Ben raises an eyebrow, but Alex looks just as puzzled. They're not expecting anyone. There's been a steady stream of people in and out today, helping them to move in. Helping wait for trucks. Unpacking. Assembling. Installing

Ben had never thought before about what was needed to run a home. Things he'd taken for granted until now. Whiteware, furniture, linen, crockery, electronic - even clothes – and every delivery had brought another spike of grief to try to ignore.

The doorbell rings again and this time Bart barks. Ben shushes him and grabs the doorknob.

"Who is it?" Jamie hangs over the banister, headphones around his neck.

Behind Ben, Alex mutters about not being the one dealing with Lucy if they wake her up. He pulls the door open and stares, open mouthed at the person on the other side, then turns and looks up at Jamie.

"It's for you."

He steps aside and let's Leo in.

***

"Ben!"

Ben glares over his shoulder at Alex. "Shh. I can't hear them."

"*Good.* Leave them alone."

"I'm not going to just –"

"Oh, yes you are." Alex grasps his collar and tugs him toward the kitchen table. "If he needs us, he'll let us know."

Ben huffs his annoyance but sits down at the table. Accepts the mug of tea Alex holds out to him.

"Didn't we pick up some whiskey this morning? I think it's in the other room, I'll just –"

"*Sit!*" Alex puts a plate of cookies on the table and somewhat mollified Ben takes one. "Eat your cookie and mind your own business."

He *is* minding his own business. His children are the most important business he has.

"That may be true," Alex concedes when he says as much, "but it doesn't change the fact that we need to let him handle this himself. "

Ben washes down a mouthful of cookie with some tea. "I feel awful. I haven't even thought to ask the kid how he's doing in days. Some father I am."

"Sweetheart, he understands." Alex leans forward and presses a kiss to Ben's mouth. "You're a good Dad."

"Did you know Leo was home?"

Alex shakes his head. "No. Don't think Jamie did either by the look on his face."

Ben glances at the door again. "Little shit better not be dicking him around, or I'll kick his ass for him."

"No, you won't. And keep your voice down."

Jamie hasn't given them any more details than he had in the car driving back from the city - though in fairness, Ben thinks, they've all been a little distracted. Based on what he does know though, Ben's still mad at Leo. After giving the case due consideration, he's decided that Leo is either trying to manipulate Jamie into doing what *he* wants, or that he wants to get the full and complete college experience. A full, complete, and varied college experience.

Ben is definitely going to kick his ass.

Alex rolls his eyes. "Really? Have you met Leo? Besides, didn't you do exactly that? Get the whole complete and varied experience, I mean. I seem to recall Polly telling me once that if you'd been straight, every girl you went to school with would have been pregnant."

Ben narrows his eyes and points his finger at Alex. "No fair quoting my grandmother at me. And I didn't have someone like Jamie at home. How are you okay with this?"

"I'm not. I don't want him to hurt Jamie any more than you do, sweetheart." Alex pushes the plate of cookies in Ben's direction. "Eat your cookies. If he wants our help, he'll ask for it."

Grumbling, Ben does as he's told before Alex changes his mind and decides he should be eating salad or something.

"What time's the meeting on Monday?" Alex stretches out and puts his feet on Ben's thigh, wiggling his toes. Ben's not fooled for an instant; Alex is just making sure he doesn't make a break for the door. Damn it.

"Ten. I'll leave here around nine and depending on what it's about, I'll call into the apartment right after and then come back down."

"Are you sure you don't want to go up on Sunday night and stay over? Avoid the traffic?"

Ben turns the suggestion over in his mind for a moment. He's done that before on occasion when he's had early morning meetings in Los Angeles but this time if different. This time he won't be able to close his eyes and imagine the kids playing on the sand. Or Alex in their bed. He shakes his head.

"No, I'll go up in the morning and I should be back by dinner." He rubs Alex's ankle. "Make me a list of the things you want me to bring back. At least I will if Ally leaves any space."

"Good idea." Alex fishes his phone out of his jeans pocket and starts tapping.

Ever since he discovered the *To Do* app on his phone Alex has stopped writing lists by hand. He says that this way he can just send them directly to whoever needs to get them, but Ben misses the bits of paper covered in the familiar block letters.

The door from the living room swings open and Jamie comes in.

"Hey, kiddo." Ben studies the teen, looking for signs of distress. "Everything okay?"

"Do you mind if Leo and I go out for a bit? We thought we'd grab a burger and go down to the beach and talk."

"Talk?" Ben asks. "Can't you talk here?"

"We can, but you're kind of making Leo nervous."

Ignoring Alex's pointed look, Ben spreads his hands. "Me? What'd I do?"

Jamie hesitates for a moment, then answers. "You're not exactly subtle, Dad. Or quiet."

Alex snorts. "Try not to be too late; it's been a long day. We'll be up for a while yet though."

"And if you need anything, just call me," Ben adds.

"Okay. Thanks." He turns to leave, then stops and comes back to the table. Hugs Ben.

Startled, Ben hugs him back. "What's this for?"

"For wanting to kick his ass."

16

After all this time Alex has long since given up trying to understand Ben's obsession with horror movies. He shifts to a more comfortable position, his head on Ben's chest, and shuts his eyes. Judging by the sounds coming from the screen, the killer has won this round.

Lulled by the sound of Ben's heartbeat, Alex runs through his list in his mind. He probably should get up and get his phone but he's warm here, curled up with Ben.

One by one, he runs through the things on the list. He needs to make an appointment to see his therapist, Ellen Jones. Talk to Ally's teacher. Bart's due for his annual visit to the vet. Somewhere in the back of his mind he has a vague recollection of either Jamie or Ben needing a dental check-up.

"Do you think the kids are okay?" Ben asks.

"The girls? Or Jamie and Leo?"

"Yes."

Alex smiles. "Idiot."

"I mean Jamie is old enough we can talk to him or he can go and see Ellen if he needs to. I'm worried about the girls though." Ben thumbs the remote, silencing the movie.

"All we can do is keep talking to them." He twists a little so he can look up at Ben's face. "How about you, sweetheart? How are you doing?"

"It still seems so… unreal. I know it happened, but I just can't believe it happened if that makes sense."

Running his fingers over the soft denim of Ben's jeans, Alex nods. He does understand. It's the same way he'd felt after Ben's heart attack.

"Do you want me to make you an appointment with Ellen?" he asks.

Ben's breath is soft and warm against Alex's cheek. "I don't know. Maybe."

"Might help to talk to someone." He lifts Ben's hand to his mouth. Kisses the palm.

"I have you to talk to."

"Not what I meant."

"I know what you meant. I love you."

Alex turns his face up and smiles. "That works out well, since I love you back."

"Even if I'm an idiot?"

"Yeah, but you're my idiot." He squeezes Ben's hand. "We'll get through this."

"Promise?"

Alex opens his mouth to do exactly that when the door opens.

Flushed and a little out of breath, Jamie hangs his jacket on the hook and goes to the armchair. Slumps in it with a soft grunt.

"Hi." He looks at the television screen. "What are you watching?"

"The Conjuring." Ben reaches for the remote.

"Nice."

Heaving himself into a sitting position, Alex lifts Ben's legs so they're across his own. "How'd things go with Leo?"

Jamie shrugs. "Okay, I guess. He says he's sorry and that he wants to try the distance thing."

"And how do you feel about that?'

Jamie toes his sneakers off and pulls his feet up beneath him. "I don't know. I want to but how do I know he's not seeing those other guys he talked about. He says he's not and that he was just being a -"

"A dick whose ass I'd like to kick?" Ben doesn't look even remotely ashamed.

"Ben!" Exasperated, Alex taps his ankle.

"What?"

"Behave." He looks at Jamie. "For what it's worth, I think he's telling the truth." He pats Ben's foot. "Come on you, it's been a long day. Time you were in bed."

Ben rubs his hands together and grins. "Now we're talking."

Muttering that he doesn't want to know, Jamie stands. Picks up his shoes. "I'm going to bed too." At the foot of the stairs, he stops. "I told him he could come over tomorrow and help me do my room, but he's kind of nervous about it."

Alex turns off the television. "I think that's directed at you," he tells Ben.

"What's to be nervous about? I'm a pussycat. As long as he behaves. "

"Dad," Jamie groans. "Please be nice."

"What? I'm always nice."

***

Stretched out on the bed, Alex watches Bart snuffle and bump his way along the baseboards, exploring the bedroom. A new basket, chosen by Lucy and Ally, is in the corner, but so far, he's more interested in his new surroundings. Every now and then he turns to look at Alex, wag his tail and give a soft woof before continuing his investigation.

Alex tucks his arm under his head and yawns. He's as restless as he is tired, unable to think of the house as home. Unable to feel the room is theirs. That will come, he supposes, and the thought brings with it a jolt of sadness. The beach house was the only place he'd ever thought of as home. The only place he'd felt safe. Loved. Its loss feels like a wound – the gaping hole left after a tooth has been extracted.

If it feels that way for him, how must it feel for Ben? Alex rubs his eyes. At least the things that made the beach house for him are still with him. Ben. The kids. Bart. Wedding photos can be reprinted. Toys, books, cars can all be replaced. Ally's awards, Polly's ancient Scrabble set - cannot.

Trinkets, souvenirs, memories gathered over the course of Ben's life - not to mention Allie's and Polly's lives – reduced to embers and wisps of smoke. Alex hasn't been able to bring himself to return again to the - what should he call it now? The site? Remains? Ben has though and yesterday he'd brought back a small lump of colored glass. Nestled in Ben's palm, it had glinted in the sun.

"From the window," he'd said in a voice thick with grief.

Then he'd swallowed and asked Alex how he was. How the girls were. Was Jamie doing okay? The same questions he keeps asking.

It occurs to Alex that maybe he should just go ahead and make the appointment for him to see Ellen.

The bathroom door opens and Bart trots over to greet Ben.

"Can't find your basket, Dork Dog?" He scratches the aging Labrador's ears. "Smell too clean buddy?"

"Come to bed." Alex pulls back the new comforter to reveal crisp new sheets. He flicks them open and waits for Ben to sit down. "Mattress is good. Should help your back."

"My back? I'm not the one who's second cousin to a Yeti and thinks running is a sane way to start the day."

"That's because it is and if you did a little more of it, you wouldn't need a firmer mattress." Alex shakes his head. "Come to bed."

He waits while Ben takes his glasses and watch off, checks his phone, and has a sip of water from his glass.

"Is this the side I normally sleep on?" Ben looks befuddled.

Rolling his eyes, Alex pulls him closer. "Of course it is. That's the side you sleep on, believe me."

"The orientation of the room is all wrong."

"The orientation of the room is just fine." He leans his forehead against Ben's. "You on the other hand I'm not so sure about."

"Nothing wrong with my orientation."

"Says you." Alex dips his head. Presses a kiss to Ben's mouth. Nips at the full bottom lip; follows with his tongue.

Ben presses against him, already half hard.

"I can't believe you bought new pajamas already."

"What else am I supposed to sl-" the words disappear into Ben's kiss.

Stretching his body out, he slides his hands down over warm skin, still slightly shower-damp. Traces the scar then spreads them out over Ben's ribs. Hard bone beneath smooth skin. Tips his head back and moans as Ben strokes the line of his jaw with short, sharp bites. Little more than the scrapes of teeth, but each sends a shiver of heat through him.

As Ben works his way down the column of Alex's neck to suck the skin at the base of his throat, Alex shoves at his pajama pants. Wants them gone. Wants to feel Ben against him. He nudges Ben's head back with his own and licks at the dip in his shoulder. The faint tang of soap stings the tip of his tongue; he sucks at the skin until there is nothing but the taste of Ben in his mouth.

Alex wants to fill his senses with him. Taste him. Smell him. Hear him.

He makes his way down Ben's chest and circles his nipple. Tongues at the stiffening nub until Ben growls and slides his fingers into Alex's hair, twisting and tugging at the long strands. His breath comes in short, sharp bursts beneath Alex as he rubs against his thigh.

Alex lets go and slides his tongue across to the other nipple. Sucks hard enough to pull a gasp from Ben. Forcing himself to take things slowly, he goes back and forth. Licking, biting, sucking.

"Fuck, baby." Ben moves against him, cockhead damp against Alex's groin.

He rolls onto his back, pulling Ben with him, fingers digging into his hips as he lifts him up so he's straddling his chest.

"Want you in my mouth."

With a low grunt, Ben steadies himself with one hand against the headboard. With the other he grips his shaft and rubs himself over Alex's mouth. Drags the head over Alex's cheek, over his lips. Back again. Sliding his hands around to grip his ass cheeks, Alex flicks the tip of his tongue out to lick at the bead of pre-cum pearling at the tip.

Heart thundering in his chest, eyes on Ben's, he takes him in his mouth and for a moment it's like the first time he did this. Everything is on fire. New, yet familiar. The sensation shakes him, and he runs his hand up until it covers Ben's heart and he can feel the reassuring, even, steady beat under his palm. The solid feel of Ben's thighs either side of his chest grounds him and he returns his hand to its starting point.

He squeezes the muscles of Ben's ass, thumbs in the cleft. Pressing at his hole. He sucks Ben's cock in deeper, tonguing the underside then circling the head.

His own cock is rock hard against his belly but for now he's happy to ignore it. To simply have the near painful pleasure of it there, waiting.

Ben whines and rocks into his mouth, fingers dropping to trace Alex's jaw, then up into his hair.

Alex digs his tongue into the slit, chasing the salty, sweet flavor of him. The strain of the last couple of weeks seems to fade as Ben fills his mouth. Hard heat… alive… real. He flicks his tongue over the head again, aware of Ben looking down. Watching him even as he gives in to the moment. Gives in to the pleasure.

Ben bucks, driving his cock further in and Alex relaxes his throat, ready for him. Even so, he feels the flash of panic at not being able to breathe and then Ben shifts back. Alex digs his nails into the soft skin of his buttocks and pulls him back again. Is rewarded with a long, low moan.

"Baby." Ben's voice is wrecked, broken. He slams back in, hard and fast, making Alex whine and shiver.

He moans around the heavy fullness of him, licks at the spot under the head that he knows will send a shudder rocketing through

Ben and is pleased when it does. Hollows his cheeks and takes him back in. All the way. Swallows around the thick heat in his throat and Ben cries out; a short, sharp sound as he pulls on Alex's hair.

"God. Fuck!" A full body shudder rocks him and he tightens his thighs against Alex's ribs. His head snaps back, mouth open in a silent roar as his muscles lock rigid beneath Alex's touch.

Alex swallows the first splash and licks frantically at the underside of Ben's cock, coaxing more from him, swallowing each burst with a low hum of desperate need.

Still holding Ben in his mouth, Alex lets go of his ass and grips his own cock. On the edge, he whimpers at the sensation as he strips it with frantic, messy movements. When Ben reaches back and rubs his thumb over the wet cockhead, it's too much. He arches up, vaguely aware of Ben slipping from his mouth, as cum stripes his belly.

Shaking, eyes screwed shut, he lies there, one hand on his softening cock the other on Ben's thigh, and for just a moment everything else disappears. There's nothing but the two of them and the way they love each other. They've made it through everything else – all the pain and the loss. His mother. Ben's heart attack. They'll get through as long as they're together.

"You okay down there?"

He can hear the laughter in Ben's voice; taps the back of his thigh until he shuffles back down and rolls away. A tissue is stroked across the mess on his skin and he smiles, eyes still shut.

"I love you," he whispers.

"What's not to love?"

The light goes out and Ben moves against him, opening his arms. Alex curls in, head on his chest, sleep already trying to take him.

"Exactly."

17

A quick look at his watch tells Ben it's nearly four-thirty. He stretches and rolls his shoulders. Grimaces at the sounds like gun shots as the vertebrae pop one after the other. Maybe Alex is right about his back.

He grabs his phone and sends a quick text to Alex to let him know he's on his way before easing the BMW out of the parking building. The box of toys and books, collected this morning, slides across the back seat and he wonders if he should have secured them better.

Carl from the car dealership brought over the keys to the glossy blue sedan on Friday afternoon, providing a much-needed break from assembling that damned trampoline. He's sure their old one hadn't been so complicated to put together.

"Use her for as long as you need to, Ben. When you're ready, come in and we'll get you fixed up." He'd clapped Ben on the shoulder and looked pained. "I'm so sorry about the Targus."

Ben had thanked him and accepted the offer of the car. He'll call him tomorrow to discuss keeping it. There are too many other things that need his attention at the moment to be worrying about looking at any others. Carl knows him well enough to have picked out something he, Ben, would normally have chosen anyway, so why complicate things?

Traffic out of the city is already heavy and he doubts he'll be home by dinner. He might make it for bedtime stories if he doesn't stop at all.

By the time the city lights are a dim reflection in the rearview, a light drizzle has started. He flicks on the wipers, adjusts the heat, and lowers the volume on the music. God, he loves having controls on the steering.

U2 cycles up on the Spotify playlist; he smiles without realizing he's doing it. The music is comforting. Familiar. It occurs to him that this is the first time since he was a child that his mother's house is not waiting for him at the end of the trip.

To distract himself from the bite of pain the thought brings, he tries to imagine what it will be like to walk into the new house. Will Dork Dog be inside in his basket or outside in the yard? There are no cobblestones, warmed by the sun, for him to lie on. Maybe he'll be in the kitchen, under the table at Jamie's feet while he sketches.

The ice-blue digital numbers on the dashboard clock confirm that the girls won't be up. They'll be tucked in, smelling of shampoo and sun. Lucy will be asleep, but Ally will probably be stubbornly refusing to give herself over to slumber until she's had her kiss goodnight.

He wonders if Alex is reading to them yet and is tempted to call him so he can listen in but decides against it. Lucy will use it as a way of staying up longer and nobody needs her cranky tomorrow morning.

Once story time is over, Alex will probably go back to the kitchen and make himself some tea. Take it to the living room and stretch out on the new sofa with notes from class. Or a book. Jamie will take the sofa unless he's upstairs studying at his new desk, but Ben doubts it. He suspects he'll find them both in the living room.

It's just… not *their* living room.

Anger, scalding and bitter, fills his nose and throat. Blurs his vision. He blinks the tears away; they're not going to help. Done is done as Polly used to say and now, he just has to make the best of it.

"Do you know how lucky you are?" His mother's voice is so clear – so real – that for a moment he almost believes she's sitting next to him. Wishes she was sitting next to him; the way she had been they'd had this conversation. "He is a good man, and he loves you so much. Do you know how few people get that in life?"

"I know." He hugs her close, hating how fragile she feels against him. "I love him too."

Allie nods. "Yes, I know. When you look at him, it shows. It makes this a little easier, knowing you have that."

"Mom…"

"Don't worry, I'm not going to get all maudlin on you." She offers him a sad smile. One filled with so much resignation that it makes him want to scream. "But it does help knowing you have him. And that he has you. It won't matter where you go, or what you do, you'll always have a home because you have each other. Even if you have nothing else." She falls silent, seeming lost in her thoughts, and just as he thinks perhaps she's dozed off because of the drugs, she speaks again. "And when this baby comes, fill your home with all the love you possibly can for her, okay?"

"I promise, Mom."

Ben rubs his forearm over his eyes. He hasn't thought of that day in years. They'd been preparing to move Allie's things downstairs, into the room that had become Jamie's, and had been waiting for Alex to come back from town.

It won't matter where you go, or what you do, you'll always have a home because you have each other.

He presses the gas a little harder.

He wants to go home.

***

He parks next to Alex's car in the garage. They need to take Jamie to find a car next weekend. Not that the kid has asked for one or complained about taking the bus. He's like Alex in that way. No demands or complaints; they'll simply accept what is and try to make it work.

Not like Ben at all.

Ben almost expects to hear Polly's laugh at that self-reflection.

"You have a remarkably well-developed sense of self preservation," she'd once said to him. "If you were a lion, you would eat all the competition."

Slinging his jacket over his shoulder, he hurries toward the house. Bart bounds across the lawn, tail wagging.

"Hey, Dork Dog." He stoops to scratch his ears. "Some protector you are. Good thing I'm not an escaped psycho."

"Says you."

When he looks up, Ben catches his breath, swamped with another wave of emotion. Alex leans against the doorway, arms folded across his chest. A smile softens his angular features. Crinkles that Ben doesn't remember noticing before, form at the corners of his eyes.

Leaving Bart to sniff at some bug he's found in the grass, Ben bounds up the steps. Drops his briefcase and throws his arms around Alex.

"Woah!" Alex takes a startled step backward. Ben clings to him, digging his fingers into the solid muscle of his shoulders. "You okay?"

"Nothing kissing you won't cure."

He confirms the statement by doing exactly that and for a heartbeat loses himself in the feel of Alex's mouth against his own.

"Well, it's not that I have anything against you kissing me but maybe we could do that inside?" Alex grins and pulls him into the house and shuts the door behind them.

"And maybe upstairs." Jamie adds without looking up from his tablet. He's curled up in his armchair on the other side of the room. "Later. Much later. When your children can't see you. Or hear you."

"How did I end up with such a family of prudes?" Ben asks as he places his briefcase and jacket on the sofa.

"Just lucky I guess." Alex smiles and his eyes do the crinkle thing again.

Ben decides he likes the crinkle thing.

18

"Dad says that if you buy anything not on the list, he's telling Uncle Matt to leave the cheesecake behind." Jamie taps a reply to Alex and puts his phone back in his pocket.

"Uh huh."

With a grin, Ben ignores the instruction and adds chocolate syrup – he knows damned well that isn't on the list – to the shopping cart and keeps walking. Can't have too much chocolate syrup at this time of year. Especially with people coming for Thanksgiving. Who knows what you might need to add it to?

Cheesecake for example.

"If he yells at me, I'm telling him what really happened to the microwave."

Wow – the kid plays mean. It's not like he'd meant to explode the thing. He'd been in a hurry was all and had simply shoved the leftovers in there – metal dish and all. As soon as he'd heard the explosion, he'd known. Thank God only Jamie had been home, and he was easily bribed with a burger and fries when they'd gone out to buy a new microwave.

And if he'd told Alex a little white lie about it having some sort of fault that had shorted it out, well that was worth the set of new paintbrushes the from the art supplies store. Jamie's had all been lost in the fire anyway.

"He's not going to yell at you."

At least he doesn't think he will. Alex has been a little… on edge lately. He's overtired and overworked and trying to juggle everything without complaint and Ben knows he needs to get him to unwind but the last few months have been frantic.

The merger settlement has cleared, and the insurance settlement has now been set for just before Christmas, so things are financially easier. Most of Ben's time has been taken up with setting up the new offices for *Crawford, Langley, and Larsen* – God, he likes how that sounds – and going up to the city for meetings and on one occasion for court. Fiona runs the new office with an iron fist. They've taken on the two young lawyers he'd sometimes used, along with a shared Legal Aide, and a receptionist.

He tries to make it home for dinner every night – even if it means working after they eat – but he knows Alex is balancing the main share of the parenting and household management. Not to mention finishing his final semester at college, juggling the two clinics, and taking care of himself. This last one, Ben knows, will be the one that gets neglected the most.

Hopefully this coming weekend will help. Matt and Claire are coming down for Thanksgiving and staying for the weekend. Ben has insisted he have the four days clear – or as clear as they can be given his role – and he intends spending the time with his family and looking after his husband.

"You know what we should get?" His eyes light up. "We should get some of that butter that's shaped like a turkey."

Jamie groans.

"It's not on the list. Dad is going to kill you. And then he'll kill me for letting you buy it."

***

Ben frowns. Why is the kitchen table covered in pots and pans? Not just one or two but, by the look of things, every single one they own. Even though there are decidedly fewer than they had before, the number covering the table is not inconsiderable.

Ally is perched on a chair at the end of the table reading a… is that a recipe book? Under the table, Lulu and Bart appear to be sharing a bowl of apple slices.

"Where would you like us to put this stuff?" he asks cautiously. Something about this scenario suggests a careful tread.

Alex drags his hand through his hair and sighs. Through gritted teeth he mutters something about anywhere Ben damned well likes.

He might be many things, but Ben is not stupid enough to take Alex on when he's got to this stage on a Saturday afternoon. He starts emptying bags out onto the kitchen counter; Jamie picks each item up and puts it away.

After a few moments of silence, he clears his throat. "Baby, what are you doing?"

"I'm trying to fit these in the cupboards without them falling out all over the floor every time I open a door." Pots are slammed one inside the other. "And the cast irons need curing."

"Of what exactly?" Alex glares at him and he holds his hands up in a gesture of peace. "Sorry. So is the problem that we don't have enough cupboards or that we have too many pots and pans?"

"I know you think you're funny, but really you're not."

Jamie winces and shoves a bag of rice in the pantry without a word. Unsure what might be a safe subject, Ben tries for something at least neutral. Window shopping motorcycles while waiting for Jamie's new Subaru to have a brake light repaired should be safe.

"While we were waiting for the car, we took a look at the Harley dealership next door. Nice bikes."

"Uh huh." Alex stacks pot lids in a cupboard, looks around, takes them out again.

"You'd look good on a Harley. All dressed in leather. Hair blowing in the wind." He ignores Jamie's eye roll and reaches for Alex who ducks the embrace.

"Yeah, I don't think so. I've seen what happens to people who come off those things."

"So, we'd be careful. I mean it's not like we'd be racing it. Just maybe take it for a spin down the coast from time to time."

"Ben, you're not getting a motorcycle."

Something in Alex's voice makes Ben put down the bag of carrots and turn around. It occurs to him that Alex doesn't realize he's teasing. And that the subject wasn't quite as safe as he'd thought.

"Baby, I –"

"No!"

Ally jerks her head up at the sharp tone and Bart appears from beneath the table. Jamie, hand still outstretched to take a bunch of bananas, freezes with his gaze fixed on Ben.

"No!" Alex repeats. "Our lives are insane enough without you wrapping yourself around a lamp post on some stupid damned motorcycle, okay?"

"Calm do-"

"Don't you dare tell me to calm down, Ben Larsen. I am perfectly calm. I just need you to act like an adult for once in your damned life, okay?"

The pot lids clatter to the floor, Alex turns on his heel and stalks out of the house. Ally flinches at the slamming of the door. Ben takes a deep breath in, holds it and lets it go again. Looks at Jamie.

"Well, that escalated quickly. Can you look after your sisters for a bit?"

"Is Daddy mad?" Lulu leans out from under the table. "What did you do?"

"No, Daddy's not mad; he's just tired." He scowls. "And I didn't do anything."

Once outside, he follows the sound of cursing to the side of the house. Alex appears to be in a battle with the hedge over the ownership of Lucy's bike – and losing. Ben reaches over him to take one of the handlebars and Alex shoulders him out of the way.

"I can do it."

Ignoring him, Ben grasps the bike and pulls it free. Wheels it to the garage and leans it there. When he turns back, Alex is sitting on the step, rubbing the tattoo on his left wrist. He goes over and sits down; closes his fingers over Alex's.

"You know I don't really want a Harley, right?"

"I know. I'm sorry."

Ben shrugs. "It's okay. You had a shitty day. I get it."

"Kind of feels like it's been a shitty year, you know?"

Yeah, Ben does know. He slips his arm around Alex's waist.

"So, do you want to tell me what the final straw was? Cupboards, pots, or bikes?"

Alex snorts. "Idiot."

"Well, in my defense, that's not exactly news." That finally gets him a smile. "Baby, what's wrong?"

"The kitchen's too small."

"Okay. That's it? Because that can be fixed."

"It's not just the kitchen." Alex puts his head in his hands. "We need to do something about that tree by the living room before every insect known to man invades. Ally asked me for a desk for her room, but I don't even know where we'd fit it. I didn't realize how small the rooms were when we looked at it. And I know she's still worried about that Logan kid."

Ben frowns. Still? They've already spoken with Miss Lassiter and the Principal. Do they need to ask for a meeting with the kid's parents?

"Maybe," Alex agrees. "And we need to sit down with Jamie and go through the college stuff but there just hasn't been time and if we leave it too long, it will be… mmmph."

Ben cuts the words off with a firm kiss. When he pulls away, Alex gives him a puzzled look.

"What was that for?"

"Seemed the best way to shut you up. What do you want to do about all this stuff?"

"I don't know." Leaning forward, Alex plucks a tuft of grass from the lawn. "The house seemed fine when we first moved in."

"Is it possible that it is actually fine and that you're just overtired? When did you eat last?"

The house while smaller than their old one, isn't small. It's just… different.

Color rises in Alex's cheeks and he studies his fingernails.

"Yeah, that's what I thought." He stands and holds his hand out. "Come on, let's go order pizza and then figure out what we're going to do about cupboards and trees and God only knows what else is buzzing around in that head of yours."

19

Alex tucks himself into the corner of the sofa with his mug of tea and a cookie. At the other end of the sofa, laptop balanced on his knee, Ben's attention is divided between whatever he's working on and yet another horror fest on television. Why Ben watches these films is beyond Alex; the man can barely look at a papercut without feeling faint.

"Why are you so obsessed with these movies?"

"I don't know - they're fun."

Muttering that Ben's definition of fun needs revision, Alex watches for a moment. Grimaces when something with fangs lunges at a young woman in a short skirt and high heels. Why do the women in these things wear such ridiculous shoes? No wonder they can never escape.

He covers Ben's feet with his own. "I'm sorry about earlier."

Ben studies him over the top of his glasses for a moment, then places his laptop on the floor and turns down the sound on the television. He doesn't, Alex notes with wry grin, turn it off. "Nothing to be sorry for, baby. How's your stomach?"

"It's fine." Smiles when Ben raises an eyebrow. "What?"

"I can think of other F words I'd rather hear you say."

"Food?"

"Among others." Ben bites into his cookie, sending a shower of crumbs down the front of his shirt.

"Bart makes less mess when he eats." He swipes at the mess with his foot. Rubs his thumb over the handle of his mug. The last three months have been hard enough without Ben worrying that he, Alex, is falling apart too. "My stomach is fine. I'm just tired."

"Can't think why that would be."

"I miss the house." He looks at Ben over the top of his mug, trying to read his face. "I know it's so much worse for you bu-"

"Woah! Back the truck up." Confusion clouds Ben's eyes. "Why would you think that? It was your home too, Alex."

Alex pulls his knees up to his chest. Ben only calls him by his name when they're in public or he's annoyed with him. "Yeah, but your Mom built it, you grew up there."

"And she left it to the both of us. We got married there. We had our children there. It stopped being *my* house the minute you walked through the door."

Fighting a rush of tears, Alex tries to smile. "It was the first place I felt safe. The first place I felt truly love and accepted. I hate that it's gone."

"Baby." Ben puts his cup down and opens his arms. "Come here."

He rocks forward onto his knees and crawls up the sofa to rest against Ben's body. Breathes in the comforting scent of Ben's cologne. Picks at a loose thread on the sleeve of Ben's blue Henley. "The framer called to say the photos are ready to collect."

"Is that what set this off?"

"No. Maybe." His sigh is muffled against Ben's chest. "I don't know. This," he gestures to the room, "is nice, but it's not ours."

"Uh… babe…."

"Yeah, I know. We bought it; it's belongs to us. But that's not what I mean." He looks up at Ben. "I miss *our* house."

Alex shuts his eyes. Listens to the beat of Ben's heart. The steady thump reminds him of what they haven't lost. Reassures him.

"I miss it too. I hate that we've lost all Mom and Polly's stuff. The kids' toys. Your books. Jamie's pictures. My suits."

Alex is about to tease him that his suits will account for half of the insurance claim, when they hear a car pull up next to the house.

After dinner, Jamie had said he needed to go to the Copy Shop in the village to print something for a school project. At the time, Alex hadn't really thought much of it. Now though he wonders what on earth was so urgent that it needed to be printed on a Saturday evening.

Jamie, a canvas messenger bag slung across his body and a long white tube under his arm, kicks the door shut behind him and hangs his jacket up.

"Get everything done?"

"Yeah, all good." He bites his lip, then in a rush of words asks, "Can I show you guys something?"

Alex sits up. "Sure. What's up?"

"You'll see."

He picks up the white tube and pulls at one end. The lid comes off with a loud pop and a roll of bright white papers falls into his hand.

"Is Leo coming home for Thanksgiving?" Ben asks.

"Yeah. He gets back on Wednesday."

"Does that mean we can expect a house guest while he's down?"

Leo hasn't slept over since the reconciliation.

"Ben! Don't be nosey." Alex taps his foot against Ben's ankle.

"I'm not being nosey. I'm being curious."

"Right. And that's different how exactly?"

Jamie coughs. "Are you two done?"

Alex elbows Ben and nods. "Yeah, go for it kiddo."

Jamie unrolls the tubes of paper. Smooths them out on the coffee table and puts Ben's mug on one corner with the cookie jar on the other.

"In my art class, we're doing a unit on buildings and Mister Daniels was telling us how most plans these days can be found in online archives. And I had this idea." He turns to face them, hands clasped in front of his knees. "It took me a couple of weeks because the plans were done before the cloud systems were around, so I asked Mister Daniels and he said to look for magazines that might have carried the plans. I remembered you said that it had been on the covers of some of the big ones." His eyes sparkle with excitement. "And he was right, that's where we found them."

"Found what?" Alex can see that they're looking at architectural plans but they're just lines and squiggles to him. Beside him, Ben leans forward to run his hand over the papers.

"Jamie… are these my mother's plans?"

What? Allie's plans? Plans for what? Alex looks at the mass of lines and squiggles again and this time they seem to make a little more sense.

"The house? These are the plans for the house?"

Jamie has his thumb almost to his mouth when he seems to realize what he's doing and lowers his hand again. "Most of them. We couldn't find a complete set and we think maybe your Mom didn't release them all. Maybe a copyright thing or… I don't know," he shrugs, "but the main house is here."

"Holy hell, kid." Ben looks from the plans to Jamie to the plans again. "This is amazing. I didn't even think about digital archives, but Mom was pretty techno-savvy – or savvy enough to know to do shit. We might be able to find the rest somewhere but even we don't – this is awesome. We should get them framed."

"Yeah." Jamie's pride gives way to something else. It takes Alex a second to identify it as nervousness. "I was thinking maybe… I could finish it."

"Finish it?"

Something in Ben's tone makes Alex turn to look at him. At the way he's looking closely at Jamie.

"Yeah," Jamie points to the sheets of paper, "see, we've only got the upper floor and some of the lower floor. Like the laundry is missing and the part where you had your desk – you know where the doors to the courtyard were? And the courtyard is just a square and your office isn't really in any of these."

"I think she added the studio on quite late. I think she always planned to have it but I remember it was built after we moved in. Maybe three months? That bit by the doors, that was meant to just be a wall and Polly convinced her to put the doors in there and make it an office nook."

Excitement lights up Jamie's face. "Mister Daniels thinks that she probably held some of the design back - or they chose not to run the complete plans – but anyway, he thinks that I could probably finish them. Or at least sketch them and then an architect could make them, you know, right."

"Okay."

There's that tone again. Alex frowns, more than a little perplexed. Jamie seems to decide something and picks up the tube again. Shakes another roll of papers out, unrolls them, and places them on top of the plans, revealing a series of sketches.

From the corner of his eye, he sees Ben's chest hitch. He covers his mouth with his hand. Alex leans forward to get a better look and finally understands what he's looking at.

There are some things that are a little different – the glass doors to the courtyard are bigger, as is the courtyard itself. Ben's office is on a different angle. The garage has moved. Despite all of that, it's still obvious what he's looking at – now that he's actually looking.

It's their house.

Biting his lip, Jamie looks at Ben. "USC has a really good architectural department."

"Yes." Ben nods. "It does."

Alex looks from one face to the other, trying to decipher what's happening.

"Your mom went there." Once more Jamie raises his hand to his mouth; this time he bites at the pad of his thumb.

"Yes."

"They have a section about her on their website." He lifts his chin, cheeks scarlet and eyes darting between them. "I kind of want to go."

"We could do that. I can phone and organize a visit," Ben says.

Alex frowns – he's not sure this is about a visit.

"No." Jamie shakes his head. "I don't need you to do that. I sent in an application last Monday. I have an interview with the Dean in a week." A shy, shaky smile surfaces. "I want to be an architect."

Alex watches Ben, who swallows several times before he finally answers.

"Your grandmother would have loved that."

20

Ben hands Claire a glass of wine. Grins and leans against the counter. They both know better than to get in between Matt and Alex as they work together, movements as synchronous as if they'd rehearsed them.

"God, I love holidays." He breathes in the rich smell of roasting turkey.

"No," Alex calls from the depths of the pantry, "you love food."

Ben shrugs and winks at Claire. No point trying to argue with that.

"You say that like it's a bad thing that I like your cooking."

"No," Alex appears with a jar of uncooked macaroni in one hand and a can cranberry sauce in the other, "I say that like someone who has to keep finding places to hide cookies."

Matt glares at him. Points to the cranberry sauce.

"No way. I brought a jar of the real thing with me." He waves a mixing spoon at a box by the door. "It's in there."

"I liked the canned stuff," Alex protests.

"Then you can have the canned stuff in sandwiches when I leave."

"But-"

"You are not putting that shit on my table."

"Actually, it's our table!"

Laughing, Ben gets the jar of sauce from the box and hands it to Matt. Kisses a spluttering Alex on the cheek as he reaches past him.

"Traitor," Alex grumbles.

"You love me."

Through the kitchen window, Ben sees Leo's car pull up in the driveway. A second later Ally runs through the kitchen, with Bart and Lucy in pursuit. They ignore Alex's request to not run in the house and the door slams shut behind them.

"I take it, everything is back to normal?" Claire pulls a chair over and sits down. Kicks off her heels and wiggles her toes.

"Well, they had lunch at Leo's place and then dinner here." Ben takes a warm roll from the basket. "I think Leo's staying the night for the first time, so I think it's probably safe to say things have settled down."

Alex takes the roll from him and drops it back in the basket. "You'll ruin your appetite."

"I'm hungry."

"Have a banana."

"I'm drinking red wine."

The thought of pairing a banana with his wine does ruin Ben's appetite. He backs up when Alex narrows his eyes and points his index finger at him.

"If you touch those rolls again, you are going to be drinking water and eating oatmeal cookies for the rest of the week."

That's just mean. Nobody likes oatmeal cookies.

***

Leaning against his chest, Lucy is already starting to doze. Ben offers her a forkful of cheesecake, but she shakes her head and burrows a little closer. He eats the morsel himself with a soft sound of appreciation.

"You want us to leave you alone with that?" Alex raises an eyebrow and both Leo and Jamie snigger. In reply, Ben digs his fork into the cheesecake again and scoops the chocolatey goodness into his mouth.

In the center of the table are the remains of the chocolate-raspberry cheesecake, two pies – one apple, one pumpkin – and a plate of salted caramel brownies. Ben has sampled all of it even though he knows Alex will insist he go for a walk in the morning and that salad, is going to feature heavily in his diet for the foreseeable future.

Totally worth it.

Alex is right – the kitchen and dining room are a little cramped. With seven of them – and Dork Dog – the room is crowded. Claustrophobic almost.

"What are you thankful for, child?" Polly's voice is so clear in his head that it could almost be real. Not a memory from the first time Alex had had Thanksgiving with them.

"I'm thankful for you, old lady." He turns to his mother. "And you Mom."

Looks into hazel eyes, full of wonder. "I'm really thankful for you, baby."

Looking around now he wishes he could show his grandmother all the things he has to be thankful for now – even if they're crowded.

Ally is showing Claire her new favorite book – something with a kid who finds a cat and they… do something together. He can't quite remember what and makes a mental note to ask her later. Matt and Jamie are discussing what studying architecture will be like, with Leo hanging off every word Jamie says. Ben actually feels sorry for the kid.

Finally, he turns to Alex, seated next to him and finds himself looking into the same warm, hazel eyes as he had that first time.

"Hey, you," he murmurs.

"Hey yourself." Under the table, Alex rubs his foot over Ben's ankle. "You alright?"

Before he can answer, Ben's phone rings. He fishes it from his pocket and checks the screen. Frowns. Lena? What the hell could she possibly want at – he looks at the time – nearly nine on Thanksgiving?

"Hi Lena, how are you?"

Alex raises his eyebrows and leans forward, both confusion and curiosity in his gaze.

"I'm sorry to disturb you on turkey day, kid."

"Don't worry about it. We've just finished eating." Everyone is silent now. Watching him. "Is everything okay?"

"Oh God, I'm really sorry, I probably should have waited until tomorrow to call you, it's just I have a problem that I'm sort of hoping you and Alex might be able to help with."

Claire takes Lucy from him. She whispers something to Alex about taking the girls upstairs and giving them baths. He stands and she pushes him back down in his seat. Ben smiles his thanks at her as Lena stutters out another apology.

"Look whatever it is Lena, just tell us and we can figure out what to do from there."

"You might want to hold off on that thought until you hear what I have to say."

Eyes on Alex, Ben picks up his wine glass and takes a sip. "Okay. I'm listening."

Across the table, Matt nudges Jamie and they begin clearing the table. Alex doesn't move, except to hand his plate to Leo. When he reaches for Ben's plate, he nods and waves it away despite the half-finished piece of cheesecake, intent on Lena's words. When she finally finishes speaking, he takes his glasses off and pinches the bridge of his nose. Tries to assemble his thoughts.

"You still there, kid?" she asks.

"You do know I'm in my forties, right?"

"Whippersnapper." She laughs, then continues, her tone sombre. "Look I know it's a lot but –"

"You're right," he says, cutting off her words, "it is a lot. Especially right now but let me talk to Alex and I'll call you back. But it probably won't be tonight, okay?"

"Of course not, it's late. Just when you can." Relief floods her voice. "Like I said, we're open to all suggestions."

Nodding, he tells her he understands, repeats that he'll call her tomorrow, and hangs up. Drops his phone on the table. Puts his glasses back on and looks around the room. Matt and the boys are gathered around the half-filled dishwasher, eyes on him.

Alex is still. Too still. Wariness comes off him in waves and he rubs absently at his wrist.

Ben hesitates, looking for the words to relay what Lena has asked.

"Ben?" Alex prompts.

"That was Lena."

Alex rolls his eyes. "Yes, that much we got. What did she want?"

A chair is scraped back, the sound harsh in the tense silence filling the kitchen. Jamie sits, silent but attentive.

Ben takes a breath.

"She wants to know if we want to foster a baby."

21

Alex swallows, unsure if he's heard Ben correctly. Did he just say Lena wants them to foster a baby? A quick look at his face confirms that yes, that is exactly what he said.

"A baby?"

Ben nods. "Yeah. You know, miniature human. About this big." He holds his hands about ten inches apart. "Costs a small fortune in diapers."

Alex scowls. "Not funny."

"Little bit funny?"

"Dad!" Jamie smacks the table making the wine glasses jump. Alex is surprised to see annoyance in his eyes. "Quit dicking around. What baby?"

Nodding his agreement, Alex folds his arms. "Yeah, what baby?"

Visibly chastened – more by Jamie's attitude than anything else, Alex thinks – Ben gulps down the last of his wine and holds his glass out. Alex picks up the wine bottle but makes no effort to pour any. Explanations first.

"Lena's been working with a special case. Nineteen, pregnant, doesn't want to keep the baby."

"And?"

The word comes out harsher than he'd intended but he's not sure he understands. Nothing about the description is, sadly, that unusual. What's more, it's usually easier to find foster and adoptive parents for babies; it's the kids Jamie's age who have trouble.

"Pour the wine."

The low, concerned tone of Ben's voice is not reassuring. Alex pours wine in both their glasses, pushes the bottle toward Matt who has taken his place next to Jamie, and picks up his glass.

Waits.

"The mother's an addict. She's been using up until about two months ago when she landed in court mandated rehab after being picked up for petty larceny. Lena was assigned to her case as part of our probono services and negotiated rehab and community service."

"How far along is she?"

Ben looks pained. "Nearly eight months."

Alex's heart sinks. "Oh God, Ben. What was she using?"

"From what Lena said, anything she could get her hands on. I kind of get the impression it's a miracle the pregnancy has made it this far."

Alex rubs his eyes. Ben's not wrong – it is a miracle.

"Apparently the last ultrasound showed the baby is developing normally – at least as far as they can tell. On the small side but they seemed to think that was to be expected. It's a boy."

"I thought babies were easy to find foster placement for," Matt says, echoing his own thoughts from just minutes ago.

Ben, Alex notes, is watching him over the top of his wine glass. He sighs. "Usually they are but this one is going to need a lot of attention. Babies born to mothers who are still using or are in treatment programs are often born addicted and go through withdrawal just like any other addict. Some of them are born with other health issues caused directly or indirectly by the addiction. That the ultrasound isn't showing anything too concerning is a good sign but until he's born, there's no way of knowing."

He rests his head in his hands, thoughts racing. Ben was talking about babies for a while but that was before the fire. Before their lives were turned upside down. Alex hasn't even thought about it since moving in here. They've all been too busy, too distracted. Has Ben been thinking about it? Is this what he wants?

"Baby," Ben's hand is gentle on his shoulder, "I'm not saying we should do this. Lena asked me if we'd consider it and I told her I'd talk to you. That's all we're doing. Talking."

Talking. Right.

So why does it feel like there's no right answer?

22

The early morning sun turns the skyline rose pink. Alex slows his pace to a jog and checks his watch. Six-thirty. The kids will be awake soon if they're not already. The sand, firm underfoot from the recent high tide, is good to run on. After weeks of running on concrete, it feels as good as slipping into his favorite shoes and feeling the tension slide from his shoulders with each step had.

Ahead the beach curves slightly. Seagulls circle and swoop; there must be fish. Their splashes break the silence. He stops running and leans forward, hands on his knees, to catch his breath. Keeps his eyes on the shells that decorate the sand in front of him as he rounds the corner.

Finally, he stops and turns to face the line of houses that edge the beachfront. There are a few more than there were when he first came down here with Ben but not so many that he considers it built up or crowded. God, that first trip seems like a lifetime ago. Would he recognize himself if he was suddenly transported back in time? That scared, lonely man who had given up on ever being happy? He's not sure he even recognizes the memory of who he was.

His gaze settles on the gap on the street. The ground is still black with soot. Jagged with debris. The sight is jarring, like a rotted tooth in the middle of an otherwise lovely smile.

Alex knows Ben comes by regularly. That he hasn't, fills him with guilt. Neither of them talk about it but Alex has seen the ash on his shoes and the cuffs of Ben's pants after his visits. Noticed the small jar in their bathroom, slowly filling with shards of stained glass. He's felt the way he clings to him in bed those nights.

Even so, he hasn't been able to face it.

Trudging up the sand, he fights a barrage of memories. Walking with Ben. The first time Ben had told him he loved him. Playing with the girls and Bart. Watching Jamie find his place with them. He stops at the top of the path, at the edge of the blackened cobbles. To his right are the crumbling remains of the studio. To his left, framed by charred posts, is the marble slab that had been the kitchen island.

He pauses where he thinks he once stood in the sun with Ben as they were pronounced married. Gingerly he picks his way through the mess to what had been – still is he supposes – the front steps. Steps where he'd met Allie and Polly. Hugged them hello and goodbye.

He stops there now, tears hot on his cheeks. This is the place where his life had changed. It had taken a single moment. He'd stood on these steps, Ben's hand on the small of his back, and Allie's kiss warm on his cheek and everything had changed.

God, he wishes he knew what to do.

Wiping his arm across his eyes, he follows the cobbles around the house and back to the sand. The sun is higher now, setting the water on fire with oranges and yellows, which seems somehow fitting.

He sinks to the sand and watches the beach come to life. A runner appears in the distance and a few minutes later passes by along the water's edge. Moments later a couple with a dog approach from the other direction. Behind him the sound of traffic fills the air.

Movement behind him makes him smile. Doesn't need to turn to know who it is.

"How did you know where to find me?" he asks.

Ben drops down next to him. Stretches his legs out– he's barefoot, Alex notices – and takes his hand. Squeezes it lightly.

"This is where we always work out our shit." Ben bumps their shoulders together. "It's where I'd come."

"I don't know what to do, Ben." He licks his lip before continuing. "I know you want to have another baby and I understand that we could offer this child a lot, but there are so many other things to consider."

"I know."

"You've just got started with the firm; Ally is still unsettled."

"I know."

"Jamie wants to be an architect and I don't even know what that entails."

"I know."

Exasperated, Alex turns to face him. "Can you say something other than that?"

Ben chuckles. "Like what? I get it, baby. There is so much more to think about than back when we decided to have Ally. Hell, there's more to think about than when we adopted Jamie. Everything is different now – and I don't just mean," he gestures behind them, "that. We're older. Busier."

"More tired."

"That too. I keep telling you that I am not saying that we have to do this, okay?"

"But you want to do it, don't you?" Alex draws circles in the sand with his fingertip.

"Honestly? I don't know. I'd just like us to talk about it but for now that's all I'm asking for."

"If we don't do it, are you going to resent me?"

"The only thing I'm likely to resent is being threatened with oatmeal cookies."

"Ben, I'm being serious."

With the tips of his fingers, Ben turns Alex's face so they're facing each other. Emerald eyes glimmer with amusement.

"So am I. If – and that's a really big if – we do this, we have to both be on the same page, just like we always are." He stands and brushes the sand from his jeans. Holds his hand out. "Come on, let's go have some breakfast."

"You came all the way over here on an empty stomach? Who are you and what have you done with my husband?" He steps closer and kisses Ben's mouth. "I love you."

"Of course you do, I'm adorable."

Alex sighs. "You're an idiot, is what you are. An adorable idiot, yes. But you're still an idiot."

23

"You did what?" Tucking his phone under his chin Ben pushes back his chair and grabs his jacket. The headache that has been sitting at the back of his head tightens its grip.

"Dad, calm down." Jamie's voice is little more than a whisper.

"Calm down? Are you kidding me?" A buzz in his ear tells him he's getting another call and doesn't even need to look to know it's from the school. "I'm on my way and for God's sake, don't call your father. He'll have a fit."

"Um, I think they might have done that already."

"Oh, fuck." Crap! That call might be Alex in that case. He checks but no, his first guess was right. The school. "I'll be right there. Do not move."

Without waiting for an answer, he hangs up and hurries from his office. Fiona meets him at the door, her face worried.

"I have to go. My son just punched some kid's father outside the elementary school."

"Jamie? Punched someone? What the hell?"

Already halfway out the door, Ben calls to her over his shoulder. "Yeah, well if I don't get there before Alex does that will be the least of our problems."

***

Ben looks around as he pulls up in front of the elementary school where Jamie was supposed to pick up Ally after school this afternoon. He spots Jamie's car a little further over and his heart sinks when he sees a police car. He had hoped to get here before them.

Alex doesn't appear to have arrived yet so maybe they didn't get hold of him. On Wednesday's he's at the Free Clinic all day and he might have his phone off. He hasn't called Ben, so that's a good sign. Well… it's a sign. Of what Ben doesn't really know.

His relief is short-lived. Alex's car turns in the school gates before he is even up the front steps. Sighing, he waits as Alex gets out and sprints across the parking lot to join him. Still dressed in his scrubs, his hair pulled into the low ponytail he wears for work, he looks flustered and a little dazed.

"I called the office and Fiona said you were on the way." He runs up the steps. "What happened?"

Ben shakes his head. "No idea. He just said he'd punched some guy out, that's all."

"They let him call you?"

"It's a school, babe, not a fucking holding cell."

A woman carrying a stack of battered-looking books clucks her tongue at them. Ben ignores her and strides down the hallway.

All Jamie had told him was that he'd been picking up Ally and Lucy up from school as agreed and had gotten into a fight with some other kid's father.

"How in the hell does a kid even get into a fight with an adult at a school when all he was doing was picking up the kids?"

That's what Ben would like to know too.

They arrive in a large reception area, lined with offices. Overhead lights bathe everything in a bright white glow that ramps Ben's headache up a notch.

Through the windows of one of the offices, Ben can see Jack Martin, the elementary principal, talking to a uniformed officer. Ben recognizes him as Rich Lewis; they've met at court a few times and Ben knows he's a good guy. Sensible and straight talking.

Next to Rich is a balding man in hornrims. His paunch hangs over his belt and his tie is loose. They can't hear him through the glass, but he seems agitated, throwing his arms around as he speaks. His shirt sleeves are rolled up to reveal thick forearms, corded with muscle. Wide gray patches of sweat stain his underarms.

Seated on the side of the room is Jamie. Dressed in his leather kilt, boots, and a purple t-shirt, peroxide blond hair tipped with blue, he looks horribly young to Ben. What he doesn't look though is afraid. Rather he's sitting ramrod straight, eyes ahead.

Ben turns to speak to the school receptionist, but Alex is ahead of him.

"Hi Annette. We got here as soon as we could. What happened? Where are the girls? Are they okay?"

Annette gives them a sympathetic smile.

"Alex. Ben. Ally and Lucy are in the library. Janie Lassiter is with them. I'll call her for you."

Janie Lassiter; Ally's teacher. Good.

Jack notices them through the glass and holds his hand up to stop whatever the discussion in his office is. Opens the door and beckons them in. It's hot inside and the air is thick with the smell of sweat.

"Ben. Alex. Thank you for getting here so fast." Ben shakes his hand as he enters. Alex does the same. "Sorry to have disrupted your afternoon."

Jamie stands. "Hi Dads. Me too."

His voice is still that strange hushed whisper. Ben frowns. The stranger makes a sound in his throat that Ben pretends he doesn't hear. Instead he focuses on Jamie.

"You too what?"

"Sorry to have disrupted your afternoon."

"What happened?" Ben looks from him to the man to Rich. He doesn't really care who answers as long as someone explains this insane situation to him.

"Ben, this is Sam Jefferson. Apparently, Jamie took a swing at him."

"There was nothing apparent about it," Jefferson says. "He punched me in the face."

Ben looks at Jamie who nods, showing no signs of remorse.

"Pretty much, yeah."

Alex comes closer. "Jamie, are you okay? You don't sound so good."

"I'm okay. Throat's a little…" he stares at the man at the other end of the desk, "rough."

"Hopefully, you've learned your lesson." The man sounds as unpleasant as he smells. "Next time perhaps you'll think twice before you try to take on a real man."

"Real men aren't homophobic douche bags," Jamie replies calmly.

"Jamie!"

Both Ben and Alex yell his name at the same time.

Jefferson lunges, lip curled in a snarl. "You little turd. I should kick your backside for you. Your so-called parents are clearly incapable of discipline."

Before Ben can say anything, Alex turns on the man.

"Excuse me? What did you just say? Did you touch our son? Hurt him?"

Ben grips his elbow and pulls him back. "Alex, stay with Jamie, I'll take care of this."

Jefferson smirks. "Oh, you're the man of the family, are you? *Top* dog so to speak." His careful emphasis on the word top is accompanied by a knowing sneer. Ben is starting to see why Jamie punched him.

"I believe my husband asked you a question. Did you hurt our son?"

"Your son. Whatever. There's no way either of you two fathered that little snot. Or those girls. It's beyond me why they let your kind adopt them though."

"Screw you," Jamie snaps, trying to elbow past. Ben hears Alex grab him and pull him back to the chairs lining the wall.

Jefferson puffs his chest out. "You foul-mouthed little deviant. Do you know who I am?"

Ben's head pounds as he pushes forward into Jefferson's space. He has at least three inches on the man and looks down into bloodshot, hate-filled eyes. This close, he can see a small bruise blooming on his cheek.

"No," he says quietly. "We don't know who you are, Mister Jefferson. Why don't you tell us?"

The flash of disquiet on Jefferson's features is satisfying but Ben knows this is far from over.

"I am the new project and logistics manager for Peters and Williams Construction. We own nearly eighty per cent of the local land developments."

That explains why Ben doesn't recognize him. He reaches into his pocket and takes out a business card.

"Well Mister Jeffersen, that's true. The company you work for certainly does own a lot of the land around San Cap. Tell Mack I said hi. Oh wait, you don't know who I am." He holds the business card up between two fingers and waits until Jefferson snatches it from him. "My name is Ben Larsen of *Crawford, Langley, and Larsen.*

And if you ever threaten our son again, I will have your ass thrown in jail so fucking fast you won't know what hit you." Without dropping Jefferson's gaze, Ben directs his next question to Rich. "Will you be pressing charges, Rich?"

"No."

Jefferson's eyes widen and his face turns a rich shade of red. "No? He attacked me!"

"And why was that?" Ben asks.

"It was totally unprovoked. That little -"

"Oh, I doubt that." Ben has a feeling he really does not want to hear the answer to the question he needs to ask, but asks anyway. "Jamie, what happened?"

"I was walking the girls to the car and this kid called Ally names because of her glasses." The words sound as if they pain him to say. As if he has a dose of laryngitis. "I told her to ignore him and keep walking. Then Mister Jefferson stepped in front of me and asked why I'm wearing a skirt."

"What did you do?"

"I told him it's a kilt and stepped around him."

"What did he do next?"

"He grabbed my arm and said to his kid that this is what happens when you let two fags bring kids up." He shrugs, still unrepentant. "So I hit him."

"You little f-," Jefferson begins but his words dry up when Rich takes a step forward.

A thought forms in Ben's mind. He looks over his shoulder at Jamie, then back at Jefferson.

"Jamie, did Mister Jefferson retaliate?"

"He grabbed me by the throat and said he was going to teach me a lesson. That was when one of the teachers arrived with Mister Martin."

Ben sends up a rapid prayer of thanks that Rich and Jack are present. Right now, he'd like nothing better than to ram Jefferson's teeth down his throat.

"Who called the police?"

"I have a right to police protection and…"

"And you felt you need protection from an eighteen-year-old who is half your size?"

"He hit me."

Rich Lewis heaves a sigh and steps forward. "After you had verbally harassed him. I suggest you go home Mister Jefferson."

Jefferson sputters, sending a shower of spit over Rich's shirt, then glares at Ben.

"I'll see you in court. You *and* your little pans-"

Shaking with rage, Ben grabs the greasy, sweaty lump of a man by the collar and drags him closer.

"If I hear you call my kid anything other than his name again, I am going to finish what he started. And trust me, I *will* finish it. As for court, you piece of shit, I look forward to it." He lets go and steps back, still shaking. "Now get the hell out of here."

Jefferson scuttles from the room, pinwheeling off the door frame and disappearing down the hall. Ben has no doubt they'll be hearing from him again but for now he can focus on getting everyone home.

He turns around and addresses Jack Martin.

"I am so sorry. Do you wish to take any action or pursue this in any way? I personally don't think Jamie was in the wrong here, but I understand that you don't really want to encourage fist fights in the parking lot."

Jack Martin sinks onto his chair behind his desk, hands raised at chest level. "No, I don't see any reason to do anything more." He rubs his mouth. "But Jamie, should that happen again, perhaps you could come and get a staff member rather than throwing a punch?"

"I'm really sorry Mister Martin. I didn't really think about it, it just happened."

Ben puts his hands on Jamie's shoulders and turns him toward the door. "Well, we'll talk about that at home. Let's go and get your sisters."

***

"Papa?"

"Hey baby girl, what's up?" Ben looks at Ally over his glasses. The ends of her hair are damp from the shower and leave little damp splotches across the shoulders of her pajamas.

"Is Jamie in trouble? For punching Logan's daddy?"

Why is he not surprised to learn that Logan's last name is Jefferson? Damn, he wishes he'd insisted on a meeting with the parents when the kid had first started bothering Ally.

"No, honey. He's not in trouble but he shouldn't have done it."

She pushes her glasses up and lifts her chin. He's struck by how much of his mother he can see in her defiance, right now and fights a smile.

"Good, because I don't think he should be. Logan is always saying mean things to people and his dad was mean too. Jamie was just trying to stop him."

Ben pulls her against his shoulder. "I know that munchkin, but it isn't Jamie's job – or yours or Lulu's – to protect Daddy and me. Jamie could have got really hurt and that would have been way worse." He kisses her forehead. "It's over now though, okay?"

"Okay. Papa?"

As much as he'd hated that she'd started calling him Dad instead of Papa, the fact that since the fire she's reverted to using it bothers him. Alex says it's normal for kids to regress a little after a trauma and not to worry too much, which is fine for the pediatric nurse who's training to be a counselor.

"Mmmm?"

"I miss our old house."

Today needs to calm the hell down he thinks as he tips her head back.

"Don't you like your new room?"

"It's okay. I liked my old one better. And I miss the beach. So does Bart."

Bart thumps his tail and whines at his name. Apparently even Dork Dog is feeling down.

"I know honey, I miss it too." He smiles at her. "Why don't we take Bart for a walk on the beach on Saturday."

A quiet woof suggests Bart votes for this plan.

"Okay." Ally twists a button on his shirt. "Can Lulu and I watch cartoons while we wait for the pizza?"

"You sure can. And I will go and see if Daddy is going to make us eat green stuff with it."

"Ewwww. No. Not with pizza. Gross."

"Yeah, well what can I say? Daddy is weird when it comes to green stuff." Especially if they're having it midweek. He stands and ruffles her hair. "But don't you tell him I said that."

Leaving her to her show, he goes into the kitchen. At the table, Alex is dabbing antiseptic on Jamie's knuckles and scolding him. The scolding might be more believable, Ben thinks, if he sounded a little less pleased with the whole situation.

A quick inspection of the fridge reveals a bottle of Chardonnay and he pours two glasses. Sits down at the table. Thinks through what he needs to say as he sips the crisp cool liquid.

Alex disposes of the cotton pad he's been using and returns to the table. Picks up his glass without a word.

Ben takes off his glasses and places them on the table in front of him.

"Jamie, please don't ever do anything like that again." He looks over at the teen and for the first time sees worry on his fine features.

"Dad, I'm sorry. But I couldn't just let him talk about you guys like that. Not in front of Ally and Lulu. I had to do *something*." He still can't get his voice above a harsh whisper.

"Look, I get it. I really do. We have all been there. But like I just told Ally, it's your Dad and my job to protect you guys, not the other way around."

"Yeah, but-"

Ben shakes his head. "No, kiddo. There's no but here. You got lucky today and to be honest that prick might still press charges." Alex startles at the words and Ben holds his hand up. "It would get dismissed but it would be a pain in the ass to have to deal with. My point is," he looks back at Jamie, "you got off lightly today. You cannot take on someone like Jefferson."

Jamie squares his shoulders. "Because I'm just a kid in a skirt?"

Alex's hand jerks, spilling wine on the table. "Jamie, that's not fair."

Ben gets up, goes around the table and crouches in front of him. "No not because you're a kid but because he's an asshole and he'd fight like an asshole." He reaches up and brushes his fingertips over the necklace of bruises forming on Jamie's throat. Notices the slight wince. "Do you honestly think he would have stopped at this if there had been nobody there? You'd be in a fucking hospital bed and that would be the best-case scenario."

Alex's hand is warm on his shoulder; he covers it with his own. "Sweetheart, it's okay. He's safe."

"I need you to promise Dad and me, you'll be smarter in the future. That you won't do something like this again."

"I guess."

"No! I guess is not good enough." Fear and anger bubble over. "Assholes like Jefferson are not worth your life, okay? Getting yourself beaten to a pulp in front of your sisters isn't smart, doesn't protect them, and it doesn't change anything. It just gets you killed. And Dad's right, that wasn't fair."

"I know, I'm sorry. I didn't mean it – I just… it's not fair that he gets to say shit like that about us and get away with it. I promise I'll try to be smarter next time."

"Kid, I can spot a loophole a mile away. You're going to have to do better than that."

Jamie's shoulders slump in defeat. "Fine. I promise I won't punch homophobic douchebags in front of my sisters again."

Before Ben can protest, Alex squeezes his shoulder.

"Ben, just take the win."

Scowling, he returns to his seat.

"Fine. And for the record, it's not a skirt, it's a kilt."

That at least gets a smile.

24

Tying the cord on his pajama pants as he goes, Alex crosses the room to the bed. Already in bed, Ben has one arm over his eyes; the other stretches out across the pillows.

"Blue or red?" he asks.

"Huh?" Alex checks his diary on the small table by the window. Looks down at the yard below and sighs. Lulu's bike is in the hedge again. What *is* that about?

It's still strange to look down and see a yard instead of the sea.

"Look, I know you bought pajamas the other day. I saw the packaging. What color?"

"How do you know they're not black? Or orange?" He slips between the sheets. Switches off the bedside lamp.

"Because I know you, baby. Blue or red?"

Alex can feel his cheeks heating up. "Blue."

Ben's body shakes with laughter. "I knew it. You're hot when you blush."

"How can you say that? You can't even see me."

"What part of I know you, do you not understand?"

"Idiot," he mutters as he rolls over.

Ben rolls with him and slides his hand over his hip. "Is Jamie's throat okay? He sounds awful."

"Just bruising I think but if he still sounds like that in a few days, I'll get him checked out." Alex runs his finger over Ben's hand. "Are you okay?"

"Yeah, I'm fine. Just… kids, right?"

Alex snorts. "Says the guy who wants more."

"Gotta stay young somehow, right?"

"If you say so." He smothers a yawn in the pillow. The adrenaline rush of the afternoon has left him feeling jittery. He should have gone for a run.

"Ally said she misses the house."

"Yeah, she's said it to me a couple of times too."

"She said Dork Dog misses the beach."

In the darkness they hear the thump of Bart's tail against the basket. Alex rolls over to face Ben. "We all miss it."

"True." Ben chews his lip; seems to be deciding something. "I had an idea and it might be nuts but I'd like to run it past you."

Considering Ben's most recent idea involved fostering a baby – an idea they still haven't made a decision on – Alex is less than reassured by the words.

"Okay."

Ben grins and kisses the tip of Alex's nose. "Don't look so worried. This place is great and everything, but I don't think any of us consider it home."

"It's only been three months." He doesn't even sound convincing to his own ears.

"True but-"

"And they haven't exactly been normal months either. I'm surprised any of us is holding it together to be honest."

"Stop interrupting and let me finish." Ben puts his hand over Alex's mouth. "Since Jamie found the plans, I've been thinking that maybe we should rebuild the house."

Alex jerks back in surprise. "What do you mean?"

"Well," Ben props himself up on one elbow, "we still own the land so we could get it cleared and rebuild. We could make some changes. Give you the kitchen of your dreams for example."

"I liked the kitchen how it was," Alex says absently. "Are you serious about this?"

"Fine you can have your old kitchen back. Yeah, I'm serious. Assuming the figures stack up on paper at any rate. One thing I thought of was, instead of rebuilding the studio we could replace it with a little guest house. That way Matt and Claire can stay with us when they come down."

"Yeah, that would be fantastic."

For the first time in weeks, Alex feels the cloak of grief slip a little. It's still there but no longer suffocating him.

"What about this place, though?"

"We have to live somewhere while the building happens and even if that goes smoothly, we're talking probably a year. We can sell it or keep it as an investment property."

"Two houses and an apartment in Los Angeles. Don't you think that's a little much?"

"See if you say that when we get the first lot of tuition fees for Mike Tyson."

Alex elbows him in the ribs. "Don't call him that." He thinks for a minute. "Do you think Jamie could be involved in the project? Like help with the plans and the designs and things?"

Ben winks. "The thought may have crossed my mind."

Of course it had. Knowing Ben, he's probably been thinking about this since Jamie showed them the plans he'd found. Alex slides his hand around Ben's neck to pull him closer. Kisses his mouth.

"Have I told you recently how much I love you?" he asks.

"Nope."

"Well, I do."

"So does that mean we can lose these things?" Ben tugs on Alex's pajama pants.

"Depends."

"On?"

"Whether you can undo the knot I made in the cord."

Growling, Ben pushes him to his back and leans in to kiss him again. Alex opens his mouth; smiles at the faint minty taste of toothpaste. He runs his hands up Ben's arms to trail them back down over his chest. Down to the trail of hair that disappears into his shorts. Knows without looking that the dark blond hair is starting to show the same silvery strands as the hair on his head, as the stubble on his chin.

He can feel his erection rests against his own, hard and hot and cups it through the cotton fabric. Rubs his thumb over the crown.

Ben presses down. Grinds their cocks together, making Alex squirm and moan. To hell with making Ben figure out the knot. He lets go of him to push his pajama pants down over his hips and wriggles out of them. Kicks them away.

Propping himself up on his elbows, Alex watches as Ben removes his shorts and tosses them to the floor. When he's sure Ben's watching, he drops his gaze to Ben's groin, licks his lips, and runs his hand down over his belly. Strokes himself with slow deliberation.

"Baby," Ben moans. Rubs his own cockhead with his thumb, then shuffles forward on his knees.

Alex opens his thighs, making room for him and draws his legs up to his chest. Holds himself open. Ben leans forward and presses his fingers to his mouth; Alex sucks them in. Laves and licks them until they're wet and saliva dribbles from the corner of his mouth.

His breath comes in short, sharp pants as Ben traces the length of his shaft, over his balls, to his taint to draw circles on the warm velvety skin before continuing down to the cleft between his cheeks.

Alex presses down with a low groan. Closes his eyes at the breach and when Ben presses in just the right spot, his hips jerk up. Pre-cum drips onto his belly. Ben adds a second finger. Small, desperate sounds rise from Alex at the increased pressure and he strokes himself a little harder.

"God, you're beautiful to watch." Ben's voice is filled with heat and need.

Alex whines as Ben pushes forward. Bears down to let him slide further in. Presses his feet to Ben's shoulders, bracing himself.

"Fuck, baby..."

"Yes, please."

Ben thrusts in with slow, even strokes. Alex meets each movement with a rock of his pelvis and a small sharp grunt of pleasure. Eyes fluttering shut, he gives himself over to sensations buffeting him. Whips his head from side to side, and digs his fingers dig into Ben's muscles with a sob of pleasure.

Ben bats his hand away and begins jerking him with sharp, rapid movements.

"Ben... don't... don't stop..." The words disintegrate into babbles as his body bucks and arches.

His back bows off the bed and thick spurts of cum burst from him as he tightens and clamps around Ben. As his body cools, he opens his eyes to watch Ben take his own pleasure, reveling in how much he loves him.

When Ben finally stills, Alex pulls his head down to his shoulder. Presses his mouth to his ear.

"You're my home," he whispers.

25

The sound of the front door slamming is followed by a volley of barks and squeals. Ben pushes his glasses up onto his head and stretches. Shopping for shoes had apparently not tired anyone out any more than this morning's walk on the beach.

Alex appears in the kitchen doorway and Ben has to hide a grin. Okay, so it might have tired someone out.

"Coffee or wine?" he asks.

"Oh God, wine. Definitely wine." Alex drops a bag on the table and sinks down onto a free chair. "Just so you know, Ally has lost another tooth, Bart is going to need cataract surgery, Jamie is on a Hello Kitty kick so don't be surprised when you see him, and Lulu apparently has lost the ability to speak at a level lower than a rock concert. Remind me again why I just did that by myself?"

"I won the coin toss." Ben hands him the wine glass and kisses him on the head. "I'll make it up to you later."

"That better mean you're making dinner and doing all the bedtime stories."

"Oh, it involves bedtime for sure."

"Uh huh." Alex looks at the papers on the table. "Did you manage to get much done?"

"Yeah, all sorted." He sits down and pats his knee for Alex to raise his foot. "Architects called."

"Yeah? What did they say?"

He slips his hand up beneath the cuff of Alex's jeans. "We have a meeting with them next week to talk over what we want. And, they said we can take Jamie and talk about how he can be involved."

Alex's face lights up. "Really? He'll be thrilled."

Ben frowns when Alex pulls his foot away and sits up, expression turning serious. "What's wrong?"

"Nothing. I just wondered something. About the house."

"Okay. What?" To his surprise, Alex leans forward and takes the hem of Ben's shirt between his fingers and rubs it. A light rose tinges his cheeks. "Baby?"

"You know how we talked about a guest house?"

"Yeah."

"Do you think we could also make some changes inside the house?" Alex's cheeks darken even more.

"Of course. What do you have in mind?"

The rubbing of the fabric grows stronger and Alex refuses to meet his gaze. "I was wondering about an extra room." Finally, he lifts his head. "A nursery."

Ben raises his eyebrows. "A nursery? Are you sure about that?"

"Not in the slightest. But when has that ever stopped us?" He sips his wine. "I thought maybe later tonight we could look at some stuff I've found on babies going through withdrawal and even if we decide it's not something we are equipped for or that it would be too much… well… there are other babies out there who need a family. Who need love."

Smiling, Ben nods. Opens his mouth to respond but is interrupted by the door flying open. Bart skids across the floor tiles as the kids tumble through yelling and laughing. He sees why Alex needed the wine.

"Inside voices," Alex pleads and drains his glass.

Ben's eyes widen as Jamie, Ally, and Lucy line up in front of him – all in matching pink Hello Kitty t-shirts. Jamie's has silver glitter around the edges.

"We got matching shirts," Lucy yells as she clambers onto his lap.

"Dad, my tooth fell out!" Ally leans in, baring her teeth to show him the gap. His stomach clenches at the sight of the wet, bloody gum.

"Leo's transferring home next year. He's going to USC," Jamie yanks open the fridge. "Can I have a beer? To celebrate?"

"Nice try. Water." Alex holds his glass out toward Ben. "I tried to warn you."

Ben tips his head back and laughs and for the first time in months, feels good. Really good.

This house isn't home – not really – but it will do for now while they rebuild something better from what they had. And it isn't his mother's plans that will make it home. It isn't the rooms. It's this. Being in the kitchen with his children and their dog.

Home is wherever Alex is.

They'll build a house together and together they'll make it home.

FIN – for now…

THANKS

I have never had a book fight me harder than *Blazing Sands* has fought me. A year long delay is unreal by anybody's definition and certainly by mine.

2020 has been for me – as I am sure it has for you – a ridiculous year and for some reason, struggling with Ben and Alex seems to sum it all up. Ending the year with finally getting them to you, also seems fitting and I can't wait to bring you Book 8.

I would like to thank May, Tom, Lauren, and Penny for their never-ending patience. As my personal life became frantic and messy, they refused to let me walk away from Ben and Alex – and they are the real reason I've made it through this mess.

A very special thanks as always to my family who have put up with my late nights, my self-flagellation as deadlines zoomed past me, and the constant cups of coffee.

To you for not giving up on me and for believing I'd get our boys over this line and ready for the next adventure, and for breathing that last necessary spark of life into them by reading – I remain forever grateful.

See you in San Cap very soon.

ARJ

November 2020

CONNECT WITH ANGELIQUE

Website:

http://angeliquejurd.com

Twitter:

@AngeliqueJurd

Facebook:

https://www.facebook.com/AngeliqueRJurdWriter/

Bookbub:

https://www.bookbub.com/authors/angelique-jurd

Also by Angelique Jurd

Jesse's Smile
Il sorriso di Jesse (Italian Edition)
The Mason Jar
Recovery
Daisy, Yellow
Belkin Lake

Joey The Complete Unabridged Story

Edelweiss Grove
Naughty & Nice
Blossoms & Bows
Truffles & Tramps
Hexes & Hugs
The Edelweiss Grove Collection Year One

The San Capistrano Series
The Beach House
Tides of Love
Winds of Change
Stormy Seas
Scattered Shells
Haunted Seas – A Short Story
Safe Haven
Blazing Sands
Peaceful Seas

The Toye Shoppe
Pet Me